I0771560

A COMPLETE LIST OF HEATHER SLADE'S
SERIES AND TITLES IS AVAILABLE AT
THE END OF THIS BOOK OR
VISIT HER WEBSITE:
HEATHERSLADE.COM

wicked winemakers

SECOND LABEL

—BOOK FIVE—

KICK'S Kiss

USA TODAY BESTSELLING AUTHOR

HEATHER SLADE

Table of Contents

Prologue

Kick

I found Isabel Van Orr on a Sunday afternoon, nine days after I'd dropped her off at the airport. Four days after her father told me she'd never arrived in Italy.

She was pruning vines in the back section of the Whitmore Estate Vineyards, five hours north of Paso Robles, wearing work clothes I'd never seen her in and an expression of fierce concentration that disappeared the second she looked up and saw me.

For a moment, we stared at each other across ten feet of vineyard rows. Her face went white, then red, then she dropped the pruning shears and ran.

"Isabel!" I broke into a sprint. "Stop!"

She cut through the vines toward an equipment barn on the far side of the property, moving fast despite the uneven ground.

I was faster.

I caught her arm and spun her around. She crashed into my chest, and for one terrible, wonderful second, every reason I had for ending things between us evaporated. All I felt was relief that she was alive, that I'd found her.

Then she shoved against my chest. "Let go of me."

"Not until you tell me what's going on." I didn't release her. Couldn't. "You're supposed to be in Italy. I drove you to the airport myself."

"I lied." She wrenched free and put distance between us. "How did you find me? Does anyone else know I'm here?" Panic flickered across her face. "You can't tell my father where I am."

"Isabel! He deserves to know you're alive."

"Then tell him that, but not where I am."

I took a step closer. She took one back.

"What are you running from, Isabel?"

"I'm not running—"

"You're terrified. I can see it. Tell me why."

She laughed, but the sound came out broken. "You don't know me as well as you think you do."

"Wrong. You're not as good an actress as you think you are."

"Why are you here?" The question burst out of her. "You made it very clear what you thought of me. I'm spoiled and—"

"When I said those things, I was angry and scared you'd hurt people I care about. And I apologized. More than once."

"It doesn't matter now." She turned away. "You need to go."

"What are you doing, working at Whitmore? If he finds out who—"

"He knows exactly who I am, and he hired me anyway." Her eyes filled with tears she blinked away. "Please, Kick. If you ever cared about me at all, just go. Tell my father I'm alive. Tell him I'll come home when I'm ready. But don't tell him where I am."

"When will you be ready?"

"I don't know."

The gaze she leveled at me was the closest she came to looking like the Isabel I'd known most of my life.

I should walk away. Respect her wishes and leave her to whatever she was trying to do. But every instinct I had was screaming that something was very wrong. That whatever had sent her here had nothing to do with her dad.

"Just go. Please."

"No," I said.

She blinked. "What?"

"I'm not leaving. You want to stay here and hide? Fine. But I'm staying too."

"That's insane."

"Probably." I crossed my arms. "But I'm not going back to Paso Robles without getting some answers. And I'm sure as hell not leaving you alone when you look like you haven't slept since I last saw you." I reached for my phone.

"What are you doing?"

"Calling Baron. Not to tell him where you are, but to let him know I'm with you."

"Kick—"

I was already dialing. Baron answered on the first ring.

"Did you find her?"

"Yes. She's safe, and she's with me."

"Where?" His words were sharp. "I'll send someone—"

"She doesn't want to come home yet. She needs time."

A long silence. "*Time*? Is this about the trust fund? Tell her if she thinks running away will change my mind—"

"This isn't about money."

"Everything with Isabel is about money. Or attention." Another pause. "What's she doing? Who's she with?"

"She's working—"

"Working?" His laugh was bitter. "My daughter has never worked a day in her life."

"She's safe, Baron. That's what matters."

"What matters is she disappeared. Do you know how that looks? Jesus, now, I have to call the sheriff and tell him she's okay." He seethed in anger. "You tell her she has two weeks to stop this nonsense and come home. After that, I'm cutting her off completely."

1

Isabel

Christmas Day started the same way every holiday did in the Van Orr household—just another day, nothing special about it at all. It was true even before my mother died.

I knocked on the door of my father's study around noon, hoping we could at least have lunch together. The house echoed with emptiness, too quiet.

"Enter," he barked.

I eased the door open just as he took a sip from a glass of wine.

Before I could say anything, he looked up from his papers with that expression I knew too well—the one that said I was annoying him.

"Sit down," he said, gesturing to the chair across from his desk.

I sat, hands clasped in my lap. At twenty-seven years old, I still reverted to that posture around him. Always waiting for approval that never came.

"What you did with the private-reserve wine." He set his glass down with deliberate care. "Do you have any idea how that made me look?"

My throat tightened. I'd known this conversation was coming. Had been dreading it since that night in the cellar when I'd stood before him, Snapper, Saffron, and Kick and admitted the truth. "I gave them the information. I helped them recreate the wine—"

"After threatening to destroy it first," he said matter-of-factly. The same way he would handle a business negotiation when someone had disappointed him. "You stood in my wine cellar and made a spectacle of yourself. *Again.*"

His emphasis on again might as well have been a slap in the face.

He leaned forward, his eyes hard. "You threatened to destroy the Hopes' last chance to save their home, their legacy."

"But I didn't," I said quietly. "I gave them what they needed."

"Only after you were caught." He turned his chair and looked out the window. "Only after you realized how much worse you'd look if you followed through. Don't pretend this was nobility, Isabel. It was damage control."

The words stung because if I hadn't overheard the story my father told about his grandmother doing the same thing, stopping the wine from being made, and the regret she lived with all her life because of it, I couldn't say I would've come forward.

He turned back toward me, and the look on his face was another I knew too well. Anger. "If you cause another scandal," he seethed, "I'll cut you off. Completely. No trust fund. No credit cards. No access to Van Orr resources. You'll be on your own."

The threat settled between us, tangible and cold. He meant it. I could see it in the set of his jaw and the way he held my gaze without blinking.

"Do you understand me?" he asked.

"Yes."

"Good." He returned to his papers. "I assume you'll be more careful going forward."

I stood, dismissed. He didn't look up as I left his study.

Back in my bedroom, I sat on the edge of my bed and stared at nothing as what my father said echoed in my head. *Another scandal. On your own. Cut you off completely.*

Everyone in Paso Robles hated me. That much was clear. I'd spent years bidding on Snapper Avila, making a fool of myself at every auction while the whole town watched and whispered. I'd threatened to destroy the Christmas Blessing Wine out of spite. I'd been cruel to Saffron Hope when all she'd done was fall in love with the man I'd never really wanted.

I was the villain in everyone's story. Even my own father thought I was a liability, another scandal waiting to happen.

But I didn't have to stay that way. I could leave. Start over somewhere else. Become someone better. Someone worthy.

A need pulsed through me with an urgency I'd never experienced. It went beyond my father's threat or the town's judgment.

I *had* to change. Had to prove I could be more than the spoiled princess everyone believed I was.

2

Kick

I got up on Christmas morning and tried calling Isabel. Six rings, then voicemail. I didn't leave a message. What could I say that I hadn't already?

It had been three weeks. Three weeks of unanswered texts and calls. Three weeks of silence so complete I started to wonder if I'd imagined the whole thing—the year of unexpected connection, the night in October, all of it.

Then last night—Christmas Eve—she'd answered, and after I told her how sorry I was, she said she forgave me in a way that suggested no forgiveness at all.

I understand. We can move past this.

She sounded cold. Like she'd given in and told me what I wanted to hear, but meant none of it.

I stared at her name on my screen. I could press call again. Listen to it ring until voicemail picked up. Repeat the cycle I'd been stuck in for days.

Instead, I tossed the phone on the passenger seat and started my truck.

I almost didn't go to my mother's house for our annual family dinner. After what I'd done—betraying Snapper's trust not once but twice, and telling Isabel about the auction arrangement that had caused all the chaos—I wasn't sure I'd be welcome. Part of me wondered if they were all hoping I wouldn't show.

But the thought of sitting alone in my house while they gathered without me was unbearable.

When I arrived, I sat in my vehicle for several seconds, my hands gripping the steering wheel. Then I saw Snapper come out the door. I got out, and when we came face-to-face in the driveway, I braced myself for him to tell me to leave.

Instead, he gathered me in an embrace that nearly broke me.

"Get your ass inside," he said when we stepped apart. "Ma's frantic."

The kitchen was crowded with my brothers, sister, and their families. There was an overall sense of giddiness in the room that I knew had nothing to do with my arrival. Then Saffron's left hand caught the light, and I went still.

"Holy shit. You're engaged," I blurted.

Snapper's grin said it all, but so did the forgiveness in his eyes. I'd been so wrapped up in my own mess that I'd nearly missed one of the most important moments of my brother's life.

The rest of the day passed in a blur of congratulations and family and trying not to think of the woman I desperately wanted to talk to. Trying not to wonder if her distance on Christmas Eve was all I'd ever get from her again.

By the time I got home, it was late. As much as I wanted to reach her, give it one more try, I went to bed instead.

But the following morning, I gave in.

I pressed call. The phone rang. Once. Twice. Three times. I was ready to hang up when—

"Hello?"

She caught me off guard. I'd expected to hear the same recorded greeting I always did. "Hey. I, uh—I've been trying to get a hold of you."

"I know."

"I hope I'm not catching you in the middle of something." I rolled my eyes. Why had I given her the perfect out to end the call, just when she'd finally picked up?

I heard rustling in the background, footsteps maybe. "I'm trying to arrange for a car service to take me to the airport."

What she said took a moment to sink in. "You're leaving?"

"I'm going to Italy."

My chest tightened. Italy, where the Van Orrs owned a villa she'd mentioned once or twice over the past year. "When?"

"My flight's at noon."

"I can drive you," I offered.

The silence on the other end went on for so long that I thought she'd hung up. I waited for the refusal, for her to tell me she didn't need anything from me, that she'd already made arrangements.

"Okay," she said quietly.

"What time do you need to leave?" I asked.

"About an hour? That should give me enough time."

"I'll be there."

The line went dead. No goodbye, no thanks for offering. Just disconnection.

I arrived at the Van Orr estate fifteen minutes early because I couldn't make myself wait any longer. My truck idled at the gate while I tried to figure out what I was going to say to her.

A year ago, we'd hated each other. I'd thought she was a spoiled princess who enjoyed making a spectacle of herself at the bachelor auction every year, chasing after Snapper as if he were some prize to be won. She'd thought I was a judgmental ass who looked down on her from my moral high ground.

We'd both been right and completely wrong.

My heart raced when the gate opened with a mechanical groan, and I drove through.

Isabel came out before I cut the engine, carrying an expensive black suitcase with her initials embossed in gold. She looked exhausted. Her face was pale in the winter light, and her movements were slow and deliberate, as though everything hurt. The cashmere sweater and jeans she wore hung looser than I remembered, and the dark circles under her eyes made her look fragile in ways that made my chest ache.

I got out and moved to take her bag. "You feeling okay?"

"I'm fine." She wouldn't look at me, her gaze fixed somewhere over my left shoulder.

I loaded her bag into the rear seat, but before I could go around and open her door, she was already in the passenger seat.

"So—"

"Kick." She turned to face me. "I really don't want to talk. I'm just not up to it."

I nodded, put the truck in gear, and headed toward the highway. The quiet between us felt oppressive, but she didn't want to talk. I doubted that meant she'd want to listen instead.

I glanced over at her and how her hands were folded on her lap as though she was holding herself together through sheer will.

As we continued in painful silence, I got lost in thought, remembering earlier this month in her father's cellar. We'd gone to retrieve the private family reserve bottles needed to complete the Christmas Blessing Wine, only to discover they were gone. Isabel had taken them.

Facing her father, Snapper, Saffron, and me, she'd broken down and confessed everything. How I'd told her about the auction—about Snapper paying Saffron to bid against her for years just to avoid taking her on a date. How hurt and angry she'd been. How she'd come to the cellar that night, intending to smash every bottle, to destroy any chance they'd have of finishing the wine.

But she hadn't been able to go through with it.

I'd watched it all unfold, knowing I caused it. Knowing my big mouth had nearly cost Saffron's family everything.

I'd tried talking to Isabel afterward. Tried to apologize for the things I said to her, to explain that I was wrong, that I'd lashed out because I knew what was at stake.

She looked right through me as though I were made of glass.

I glanced at her now. She was staring out the window, her profile sharp against the gray sky. The Isabel I'd known—the one who'd sat with me in that bar a year ago and let her walls down—felt distant. Unreachable.

Things between her and me had changed after last year's Wicked Winemakers' Ball. I'd gone to a bar after the annual fundraising event, needing a drink and some distance from the circus. The bachelor auction my sister—the ball's chairperson—forced me to participate in always left me tense. I hated watching my brothers and friends paraded around while women bid ridiculous amounts of money for the privilege of one date. More, I hated having to do it myself.

A half hour later, I was on my second beer when Isabel walked in. The red gown she'd had on earlier was gone, traded for jeans and a sweater. Her hair hung loose around her shoulders instead of being pinned up in the elaborate style it had been in. We'd sat on opposite ends of the bar at first, both pretending the other didn't exist.

But she didn't leave. And eventually, I gave in and moved to the stool beside her.

At first, we bickered with the same rhythm we always did—sharp and cutting. Then she ordered another glass of wine, and I made some comment concerning her bidding on Snapper again. Instead of the snippy comeback I expected, her shoulders dropped like the fight went out of her.

"You want to know the real reason I do it?" She turned to look at me, and her eyes were different. Vulnerable in ways I'd never witnessed. "It's not about Snapper. It's never been about Snapper."

I waited, unsure where this was going.

"It's about *winning*." She laughed, but the sound was hollow, empty of humor. "Pathetic, right? I have money, status, all of it, and I'm spending thousands of dollars a year just to feel as though I'm not invisible."

The admission hit me hard. Because I'd seen it then—her loneliness and the practiced smile she showed everyone while connecting with no one. The daughter raised by boarding schools and absent parents, shipped off so they could travel the world without the burden of a child.

She tucked a strand of blonde hair behind her ear, and the gesture was so unguarded, so unlike the polished princess everyone else saw, that my entire perception of her shifted in that moment.

"You're not invisible," I said.

She met my eyes and held my gaze. "Yes, I am. Why do you think I'm sitting alone in a bar?"

That night had started something neither of us understood. Over the next year, we'd stayed in occasional contact. A text when one of us thought of the other. A conversation when I was in town between rodeos. Nothing serious or complicated, just an unexpected connection neither of us wanted to let go.

Until the day after the same event this year, when I'd destroyed it by saying things I couldn't take back.

"How long will you be in Italy?" I asked when we were halfway to the airport.

"I don't know. A while," she said quietly.

What did that mean? A week? A month? Longer?

I wanted to bring up Christmas Eve, to understand why she'd said she forgave me when she clearly hadn't. To explain in a way that might actually reach her this time. "When I said I was sorry—"

"I forgave you." Her words were clipped. "Can we leave it at that?"

I backed off, but my mind kept going back to this year's ball. It was held in mid-October, after most of those in the valley had finished harvesting their grapes.

The tension between us at the auction had been electric, crackling in the air every time we ended up near each other. Whenever I'd looked across the room, she was watching me. Then, when she'd turned away, I tracked her movements, unable to stop.

The following night, she'd shown up at my house unannounced, asking if we could talk. The door had barely closed before we were tearing at each other's clothes. A year of wanting, of dancing around what was building between us, and suddenly there was nothing holding us back. Her hands shook as she grabbed at my shirt. My fingers fumbled with the zipper of her dress.

We barely made it to the bedroom. The need was overwhelming—frantic, urgent, and consuming. I'd spent a year trying not to think about this, about her, and now that I had her, I couldn't get enough.

When it was over, we lay tangled in my sheets, breathless and stunned by what we'd just done. She'd traced patterns on my chest with her fingertips while I memorized the feel of her in my arms.

We'd barely slept, but when the sun rose, everything between us shattered.

I'd gotten up to make coffee, trying to figure out what would happen between us now. When I returned to the bedroom with a cup for each of us, she asked about the rumors swirling around the Christmas Blessing Wine. She wasn't accusatory, instead she appeared curious. I told her about the foreclosure Hope Winery was facing, how Saffron came up with the idea that recreating the wine from 1955 might bring in enough money to save them, and that in exchange for bidding on him, Saffron wanted Snapper to help her.

Then she'd asked a question I never should've answered.

"Why did Saffron bid seventy-five thousand dollars on Snapper at the auction if her family's broke?"

I'd responded without thinking. Without considering what the truth would do to her. "She doesn't pay. Snapper does. Every year. So he doesn't have to go on an actual date with anyone."

The color had drained from her face as understanding crashed down on her.

"Anyone," she'd whispered. "You mean me."

"Isabel—"

"Years of bidding. Years of everyone watching. And it was deliberate." She'd stood and wrapped a blanket around herself. "The whole town laughing at desperate Isabel Van Orr, and you all made sure I'd keep coming back for more. Made sure I'd embarrass myself over and over."

"It wasn't like that."

"What was it, then? Because from where I'm standing, it looks exactly as it is—public humiliation for everyone's entertainment."

While it was about Snapper not wanting to have to take someone on a date—namely her—I wouldn't have gone so far as to say it was about intentionally humiliating her. Except I had no defense that didn't sound hollow.

She grabbed her clothes and went into the bathroom.

"You want to know what's funny?" she said when she came out dressed, and clearly angry. "I actually found information that could help Snapper and Saffron. Details in my grandmother's papers, concerning what was missing from the recipe."

I went still. "Isabel—"

"But I'll never give it to them. Not after this." She looked at me with tear-filled eyes. "This is what they both deserve after what they've done to me."

And that was when I'd said things I couldn't take back. Things that had been eating at me for two months.

"This is exactly what everyone says about you. You're a spoiled brat who only thinks of herself. Someone tries to be real with you, and you threaten to destroy the good in other people's lives because your feelings got hurt."

She'd gone pale. Every insecurity I'd learned in that bar a year ago—every fear she'd confessed when her walls were down and she'd trusted me with the truth—I'd weaponized. I'd thrown them in her face because I was panicking and defensive and too stupid to see what I was doing until it was too late.

She'd grabbed her purse and headed down the hall.

"Isabel, wait—"

But she was already gone. The door slammed behind her hard enough to shake the frame.

I'd let her go. And I'd been paying for it ever since.

When the airport exit appeared ahead, the ache in my chest worsened. Isabel was leaving, and I had no idea how to stop her. Or get her to listen to my apology again. Really listen.

I stopped at the departure curb and put the truck in park, but neither of us moved. The engine ticked in the sudden stillness, and when she reached for the door handle, I got out and retrieved her bag from the backseat.

We stood on the sidewalk, facing each other. Her blonde hair was up in a tight bun, like it usually was, accentuating the exhaustion etched into every line of her features. She looked as though she hadn't slept in weeks. As though something was eating her alive from the inside.

"Thanks for the ride." She spoke politely. Like we were strangers.

I wanted to say something that would make this hurt less for both of us. The thing that would give us both a reason to try again. "Take care of yourself," was all I could come up with.

She nodded and reached for the suitcase handle. Our fingers brushed for half a second, and she yanked it away as though I'd burned her.

"Goodbye, Kick."

She walked toward the terminal entrance, rolling the suitcase behind her, and I watched her go, waiting for her to look back. Hoping she would.

She didn't.

The automatic doors swallowed her, and she was gone.

The drive home felt twice as long. Every mile doubled on a highway that was an unfurling gray expanse ahead of me.

Her farewell replayed in my head. It had sounded permanent. Final. As though she was closing a door and locking it behind her, throwing away the key so neither of us would be tempted to open it again.

She'd mentioned the Van Orr villa in Italy once or twice, and it sounded beautiful. There were sprawling vineyards, centuries-old stone buildings, and views of the Tuscan hills that went on forever.

When there, she could distance herself from her father's emotional coldness, from Paso Robles gossip, and now, from me. From the mess I'd made of us.

Maybe that was what she needed. Space to breathe without judgment crushing her. Distance from the person who'd hurt her most.

We were never going to work anyway. Van Orr and Avila—both from wine country families, but we'd chosen such different paths. She'd stayed in the world she was born into, navigating the social circles and expectations. I'd chosen rodeo over the family business, spending most of my time on the circuit and traveling from town to town.

I thought of calling Snapper. He wasn't just my brother; he was my best friend. My hand even reached for my phone, but I changed my mind and left it in my pocket.

How would I explain how I was feeling? That driving Isabel to the airport had left me feeling hollowed out? That I'd spent two months trying to fix what I'd broken, only to watch her walk away without looking back? That the woman everyone thought was a spoiled princess chasing my brother was actually the only person who'd ever really seen me?

Snapper would never understand. He'd never seen what I saw in her. No one had except me.

By the time I got home, I'd convinced myself this was the right ending. The only one that made sense.

Italy would be good for her. Time away from the town that had laughed at her for years.

I hoped she found whatever peace she was looking for over there.

Even if it meant I never saw her again.

3

I stood at the airport departure gate, watching planes take off through the floor-to-ceiling windows. Kick had dropped me off at the curb an hour ago.

I'd lied and told him I was going to Italy. The same thing I'd told my father.

The guilt of those mistruths pressed against my chest, but what else could I have told them? The truth? That I was running away to the Russian River Valley, hoping to start over? That I needed to disappear before anyone discovered my secret?

While my father wouldn't have bothered, Kick would have asked questions I couldn't answer. So I'd let him believe the lie.

Instead, I'd bought a ticket to San Francisco and checked my single suitcase. I'd liquidated what I could from my personal accounts before my father could freeze them. It wasn't much—he'd never given me full control of my trust fund, always keeping me dependent. But it would be enough to get me through a few months if I was careful.

My phone buzzed with a text from my father. *Let me know when you arrive.*

I stared at the message for several seconds, trying to decide whether or not to respond.

I eventually turned the phone off. My guilt twisted tighter, but I forced it down. This was survival. Self-preservation. If he knew where I was really going, he'd find a way to interfere. To control me. To remind me that I was his daughter and Van Orrs didn't run away from their responsibilities.

But I wasn't running away. I was running toward something. A fresh start. A chance to prove I could be more than my last name. More than the spoiled princess everyone saw when they looked at me.

I'd heard through the wine industry grapevine—the network of gossip and information that flowed through every tasting room—that the Whitmore family was looking for a marketing director. Marketing had been my degree, though my father never took it seriously.

"You don't need a job," he'd said when I graduated from Berkeley. "You're a Van Orr. That's enough."

As if I didn't need purpose or meaning beyond being his daughter.

My timing was absurd, showing up, looking for work, during the holidays. But where else could I go? And there was a certain poetic justice in it—Thomas Whitmore and my father had had a massive falling out five years ago over a piece of property. Some bitter dispute neither would ever forget. He would never contact my father. Would never reveal where I was. I'd be safe there. Hidden.

When the boarding call came over the speaker, I picked up my carry-on and joined the line of passengers shuffling toward the gate.

Kick's face flashed through my mind. How he'd looked at me before he drove away—concerned, confused, searching for answers I couldn't give him. He'd seemed to be memorizing every detail of my face, as if he knew something was wrong.

The other thing that kept replaying in my mind, that hadn't stopped since our one night together, was the way he'd kissed me. None other had made my toes curl or heat spread through my body the way his did. It was like a promise. I used to wonder if that kind of kiss even existed outside of books and movies—the kind that made you feel seen, cherished.

I forced the thought away before it could take root. Kick Avila had made his choice the following morning when he called me a spoiled brat who only cared about herself. When he'd made it clear that any feelings between us—if they'd ever existed—were done.

He'd treated me the way everyone else did. Like a disaster. A liability. Someone who hurt people without meaning to and caused chaos wherever they went.

Maybe this fresh start would change that. Maybe it could be the place where I figured out how to be someone worth knowing. Someone who built things instead of destroying them.

The plane lifted off, and I watched Paso Robles disappear beneath the clouds.

I landed in San Francisco, rented a car, and drove to the Russian River Valley. It took less than two hours, winding through hills covered in winter-bare vineyards. The landscape reminded me of home—rolling terrain, neat rows of dormant vines, and the occasional stone winery tucked into a hillside. But this wasn't home.

This was somewhere I could be mostly anonymous. Somewhere few knew my history or my mistakes.

The rental cottage I'd found online was small but clean. I unpacked my suitcase, trying not to think about my father's threat or the precarious future I was constructing.

Instead, I re-read the email I'd drafted last night.

Dear Thomas,

I understand you're looking for a marketing director for Whitmore Estate. As Sebastian may have told you, I have a degree in marketing from Berkeley, and as you know, I grew up in the vines. I'd like to discuss the position with you at your earliest convenience.

I'm currently in the Russian River Valley and available to meet in person.

Best regards,

Isabel Van Orr

My finger hovered over the send button. This was it. The moment where I either committed to this new path or backed out and slunk home to face my father's judgment.

I hit send before I could second-guess myself.

The response came faster than I expected. Twenty minutes later, I received a reply, not from Thomas, but from his son Sebastian, who everyone called Bas.

Izzy! You're here? Tried to call, but got your voicemail. Ring me, sweetheart. I can't wait to see you.

Bas had always been like this—excited to see me and genuinely happy when I was around. We'd been friends since we were kids, back when our fathers were close too. And our mothers. Tragically, his mom passed away three months after mine had. It was something else he and I had bonded over.

The other positive thing about being here, about potentially working for Whitmore, was my relationship with him. He'd always liked me exactly the way I was. Our friendship was unconditional, and right now, I needed that more than ever.

I turned my phone on and called him.

"Man, is it good to hear your voice. What are you doing here? Wait, don't answer that. What are you doing *right now*?"

I laughed inwardly at his exuberance. Like his unconditional acceptance, I needed someone who was excited to see me. "Nothing at the moment."

"Do you have plans for dinner?"

I checked the time, surprised to see it was almost six. "I'll probably just grab something simple in town."

"Not a chance, Isabel. Dad and I are here alone, and dinner is almost ready. Get on over here. Wait, do you need a ride?"

I chuckled again. "No, I have a car."

"How long will it take you to get here? We'll hold off eating."

I told him I'd be there in ten minutes, and when I arrived, Bas met me at the door before I could knock. He hugged me hard, and I let myself enjoy how good it felt.

"You look exhausted," he said, studying my face.

"Long day." I smiled. "Long week, actually."

"Come on. Dad's inside. He'll be thrilled to see you."

I followed him through the house, taking in the warm wood floors and the photos lining the walls. The Whitmore family looked happy in those pictures. Bas and his four siblings at various ages and their mother, Kim, smiling in all of them. A family that clearly loved each other.

His father stood when we entered the dining room.

"Isabel, welcome. This is an unexpected surprise." His expression shifted from curiosity to genuine warmth before he embraced me the same way Bas had. He was in his late fifties, with silver threading through his dark hair. Unlike my father, his presence was commanding without being intimidating. He'd aged since I last saw him, but he still had that sharp intelligence in his eyes that had made him one of the most respected figures in the wine industry.

"I hope I'm not intruding."

"Are you kidding? You're welcome here any time. You know that, right? What happened between your father and me has no bearing on how important you are and always have been to our family." He looked over at Bas, who draped his arm around my shoulders.

"Izzy's looking for a job," he blurted.

I elbowed him. "Bas!"

"Is that so?" Thomas asked.

"Yes, but I'd hoped to handle our discussion about it professionally rather than crashing your dinner."

"Come on. Let's have a seat. We'll eat, and you can fill me in on what's going on in your life."

I settled into the chair, grateful when Bas poured me a glass of water when I rested my hand over the wineglass.

After a few minutes of small talk—memories of past holidays, updates on Bas' siblings—he grinned at me across the table.

"Remember when we were kids? Years ago, before everything went sideways between our families?" He shook his head, still smiling. "We had some good times at Miremont."

Something tightened in my chest. Miremont had belonged to my mother's parents. It was the one place that was supposed to be mine.

"My father sold it," I said, steeling my emotions. If I started to cry, it would be impossible to stop. Few things hurt as much as what my father did with that property.

Bas' brow lifted. "He sold Miremont? I didn't know that." He studied me, clearly wanting to ask more, but something in my expression must have warned him off. "I'm sorry, Izzy. I know how much it meant to you."

I shrugged, not knowing how to respond. It had been five years, and the wound still felt fresh.

Thomas cleared his throat gently, steering us to safer ground. "I don't want to make you uncomfortable, Isabel, but does your father know you're here?"

"He does not," I admitted. "We had a…falling out, so to speak."

He nodded like he understood—because he did.

"I've decided I need to make some changes in my life. Start fresh somewhere new."

"What kind of changes?" he asked as he cut into a piece of chicken.

"I need to work. Actually work, not sit on charity boards and smile for photos." The words came out more forceful than I'd intended, but I didn't try to soften them. "I have a degree in marketing from one of the best schools in the country, and I haven't been able to use it like I want to."

"Let me guess. Your dad patted your head and told you to run off and look pretty?" He shook his head. "I'm sorry. That wasn't fair. Feel free to kick me under the table if I say something like that again."

"It's true enough," I muttered, meeting his gaze directly. "He's never taken me seriously. Not that it's entirely his fault."

"Yeah, it is," Bas chimed in.

"That's enough, Sebastian," his father warned.

"Look, I meant it when I said I wanted to handle this professionally. Can we set up a time for an interview? I mean, if the position is still available and you're interested in what I can bring to the table."

"Dad—"

Thomas raised his hand. "I know exactly what you bring to the table. No one understands how a winery operates better than someone who grew up living and breathing the vineyard. I'm also familiar with Berkeley's Haas School of Business. Their marketing program is top-notch. Ranked among the highest in the country."

"Yes, sir," I said.

"Tell me about Whitmore. How you see it."

"It's one of the oldest wineries in the Russian River Valley. Established in 1934 by your grandfather. You're known for your award-winning Pinot Noir and Chardonnay, and you've built a reputation for sustainable practices and innovation while respecting tradition." I took a breath, and a smile tugged at the corner of Thomas' mouth.

"Weaknesses?"

"Legacy wineries assume their reputation speaks for itself, but if millennials have never heard of you because you're not where they're looking, your history doesn't matter."

"See?" said Bas.

Thomas cocked his head in his son's direction. "Let the woman talk." His gaze returned to mine. "What else?"

"You're competing against boutique wineries that tell compelling founder stories and make customers feel part of something exclusive, while you're trading on a legacy that feels more like a history lesson than a lifestyle brand."

"Interesting observations," he said.

Before he could ask another question, I continued. "Those are generalities. Easy ones. But for me to really understand what Whitmore is up against, I need to learn this place from the ground up. Literally. I'd want permission to work in the vineyard, to get to know your process from vine to bottle. I don't want to market the wine in a vacuum—I need to know it. Understand it in ways that will make my work authentic."

Thomas exchanged a glance with Bas, and silent communication passed between them, father and son understanding each other without speaking.

"That's an unusual request," he commented.

"I know. But I'm serious. About all of it." My eyes bored into his. "I need this chance, Thomas. I need to prove I can be more than my last name."

My blunt honesty surprised even me. But they were true. Truer than anything else I'd said.

He was quiet for several seconds, then he nodded. "You're hired."

It took a second to register. "Seriously?"

He laughed. "Yes, Izzy, seriously. You can start after the new year. Bas can give you an overview of the vineyard operations. We'll draw up a formal contract in the meantime, with a standard starting salary and benefits package."

When I reached over and touched his hand, my heart was pounding so hard I was sure they could hear it. "Thank you. You won't regret this. I promise."

"I know I won't." His smile was kind. "Where are you staying?"

"A short-term rental. A cottage a few miles from here. I'll need to find something more permanent eventually, but it'll work for now."

"We have guest cottages on the property," Bas said, looking to his father for confirmation. "Three of them. Empty this time of year. You could stay in one of those."

I looked between them, not quite believing what I was hearing. "Are you sure? I don't want to impose—"

"You're not imposing," Thomas said firmly. "Consider it part of the employment package. Bas will show them to you tomorrow morning. Pick whichever one you prefer. They're all furnished, utilities included."

His generosity overwhelmed me. I'd come here expecting to beg for a chance, to grovel and plead. Instead, I'd been given a job and a place to live.

"Thank you," I said again. "Really. Thank you both."

I drove back to my rental cottage two hours later, processing everything that had happened. The conversation had stretched on after dinner. Bas filling me in on their winery operations until Thomas announced that was enough shop talk for the night.

The best part was that they'd both treated me as a colleague. Someone whose opinion mattered.

Now, lying in an unfamiliar bed, I stared up at the dark ceiling. I should've felt relieved, but there were other things preventing me from relaxing.

The lie about going to Italy was merely the beginning. The rest of it—the other lies and secrets—would hurt both my father and Kick so much more if they found out. *When* they found out.

I had to hope that, by then, I'd be strong enough to face whatever came next.

4

Kick

I got home a few minutes after one in the afternoon. The drive back from the airport had taken less than an hour, but my hands hurt from gripping the steering wheel, and my jaw ached from clenching it the entire way.

Isabel was gone. On a plane to Italy. Walking away without looking back.

I sat in my truck, staring at my house, before cutting the engine. For the past few years, I'd been gone far more than I was home while Snapper and I chased the team-roping championship at every rodeo we could get to. Coming back to an empty house had never bothered me before.

It bothered me now. Maybe because I wouldn't be heading out again any time soon. The companionship, the parties, and the women were now a thing of the past. Snapper's shoulder injuries had sidelined both of us, and while he'd told me it wouldn't bother him if I found another header, I never would. Snap and I had been a team since we were kids. It would take years to develop the same intuitive approach he and I had when it came to roping a steer in under four seconds. Hell, I'd heard someone just did it in three point two. No way we'd come close to that, especially at our ages. I'd turned thirty a couple of months ago, and Snapper was two years older than me. The two guys who won this year's NFR were both twenty-three. Sure, there were guys older than us who still competed and made damn good money at it. But with every passing year, the injuries happened more often and got worse. Just like my brother's.

What I hadn't figured out yet was what the hell I'd do with the rest of my life. I could work at our family winery full-time. I helped out whenever I was home. It was good, honest work, and I loved being in the vineyards, but as the youngest of seven, I wouldn't be in the running for head winemaker until I was in my seventies. Not that I aspired to be. That was the problem. Other than being a roper, I hadn't aspired to a damn thing.

I forced myself out of the truck and went inside, where the silence pressed against my eardrums and thoughts of Isabel swirled around in my head. Why had she looked like she was going to a fucking funeral rather than her family's swanky villa in Tuscany? I tried to shake my worry. She was fine. Not thinking about me—or us—at all. Then again, I was doing enough of that for her and me combined.

So why did my gut keep insisting something was off?

I dug out my phone and opened Instagram. Her last post was from three days ago—wine bottles at the Van Orr estate with some caption about holiday vintages. I scrolled through her feed, looking for updates. Airports. Planes. Italy.

Nothing.

Maybe she just hadn't posted yet. The flight was long, and she'd just gotten in the air. Or maybe she'd outgrown social media like most of us had.

I closed the app and tossed my phone on the counter.

The rest of the day dragged. I unpacked my bag from Christmas. Did laundry. Fixed the fence in the backyard that had been sagging since November. Anything to keep my hands busy and my mind off Isabel.

It didn't work. Even after I finally went to bed, sometime around two, she plagued my dreams.

The following day, Snapper called and asked if I wanted to help at the vineyard. Relief hit me before I even answered. Two days ago, my brother and I weren't speaking. Now, he was inviting me back to work alongside him like he used to.

"Yeah," I said. "I'll be there in twenty."

We worked side by side, and while the rhythm was familiar, there was a carefulness between us that hadn't been there before. Like we were both aware we'd almost broken something we couldn't fix. He didn't push for conversation, and neither did I. Being together was enough. The easy comradery would come back on its own if we didn't try to force it.

Physical work helped. My shoulders ached by midday, and my hands were raw despite the gloves. Physical pain was easier—it made sense in a way heartbreak didn't.

"You staying for dinner?" Snapper asked as we loaded tools into the truck bed. "Ma's making tamales."

"Not tonight."

"Why not? They're your favorite."

"Tired, I guess."

He studied me. "When was the last time you had a decent night's sleep?"

"Don't know." I didn't say it, but it felt like it had been weeks.

"Come up to the house. Ma will give you some to take with you."

I shook my head. "She'll try to talk me into staying."

"You're right. I'll bring some over to you later."

"You don't have to do that."

He smiled as if he couldn't help himself. "I'll be there anyway. Saffron's moving in tomorrow. Permanently."

I reached out and squeezed his shoulder. "I'm happy for you, man. Have you set a wedding date yet?"

He cocked his head and looked at me like I'd grown an extra one. "We've been engaged less than a week, Kick." He nudged me with his elbow. "Go sleep. Take something if you have to. I'm worried about you."

Exactly how exhausted I was became apparent almost immediately when I felt myself tearing up. Which, of course, my brother noticed.

"See ya later, Kick," he said as he walked toward the house and I went in the direction of my truck.

December twenty-eighth and twenty-ninth passed the same way. Work at the vineyard. Come home. Think about Isabel. Try to sleep. Toss and turn instead. Rinse and repeat, as they say.

New Year's Eve arrived cold and clear. The big auction was tonight—the culmination of everything Snapper and Saffron and, at the end, Isabel had worked on. The Christmas Blessing Wine would be sold, and the Hope family's foreclosure would be paid off. Everything they'd fought for would come together.

I should skip it. Let Snapper and Saffron have their moment without me hovering in the background. But Ma had made it clear that all the Avilas were expected to attend, and I wasn't ready to explain why I wanted to stay home.

I showed up at the venue just after seven. The place was packed—wine industry elite from around the world were dressed in their finest, ready to bid on history. Bottles of the legendary wine sat on display at the front of the room, catching the light.

I found Snapper near the bar. He looked good. Happy. Saffron stood beside him, her hand in his, and the way they looked at each other made my ribs ache.

"Didn't think you'd come," Snapper said.

"Ma would've killed me if I didn't."

He laughed. "True."

We talked about nothing important while people filed in and found their seats. I scanned the crowd out of habit, looking for familiar faces. Everyone we knew was here, along with a whole lot of people we didn't.

I noticed Baron Van Orr standing near the front, talking to another winemaker, Malcolm Warwick. He looked the same as always—expensive suit, cold expression, the posture of a man who owned everything in sight. I wondered if he'd heard from Isabel. But as much as I wanted to ask, I couldn't think of a good enough reason to bring it up that wouldn't make me look like a lovesick idiot. Which I was, not that I wanted anyone to know that.

The announcements were made. The auctioneer went through the preliminaries, building anticipation for the main event, and when he finally brought out the first lot, the room went quiet.

Bidding was fierce. The numbers climbed fast—not that I was paying attention.

Originally, when Saffron came to Snapper for help, she'd proposed a partnership. The Hope family would take half the earnings, and the Avilas the other half. When the Van Orrs got involved, that split became complicated. It was quickly resolved when Brix, my oldest sibling, who'd stepped into the role of family patriarch when our dad died suddenly when I was just a kid, suggested that everything beyond the Hope's cut should be given to charity.

We'd taken a family vote, the support for Brix's idea was unanimous, and when he presented the plan to Baron, he was all for it too.

By the time midnight rolled around, the auction had long since ended and most of the guests had left. Only a few of us remained, mainly family.

Deciding there was no reason for me to hang around any longer, I walked over to Snapper and Saffron. "Hey. I just wanted to say congratulations again. Tonight was incredible."

"Thanks." My brother's eyes scrunched when he looked into mine. "You okay?"

"Yeah, I'm good. Just—" I paused. "I'm really happy for you both. The way you brought all that together, the wine, the auction, everything."

"We couldn't have done it without you," said Saffron. "Without everyone."

I was about to argue and say I didn't do much when Baron approached.

"Sorry to interrupt, but, Kick, have you heard from Isabel?" he asked.

"No, not since I took her to the airport a few days ago. Why?"

"Did she say where she was going?"

"Your villa in Italy. I assumed you knew. Is something wrong?"

Baron's face went pale. "She never arrived."

"What?" I asked as a feeling of dread washed over me.

"I've been unable to reach her, so I contacted the caretaker this morning. She isn't there." He sounded controlled, but anger simmered underneath. He leveled a look he was well-known for at me. All intimidation. "Where is she?"

I shook my head while my mind raced. "No idea. Like I said, I dropped her off at the airport. That's the last I saw or heard from her." While I hoped I sounded nonchalant about it, I was anything but.

Baron's jaw clenched. "If you hear from her, you'll let me know immediately."

It wasn't a question.

He walked away before I could respond.

I felt the world tilt sideways.

If Isabel never arrived in Italy, it either meant something had happened to her or she'd lied. To me and to her father.

"Kick? What's going on?" Snapper asked.

"I'm not sure, but I've had a bad feeling since I watched Isabel walk into the airport terminal."

Both his and Saffron's eyes opened wide. "What are you thinking?" my brother asked.

"I have a request."

Snapper nodded, picking up on where I was headed without my needing to say it. He whispered something in Saffron's ear. She nodded, hugged me, then went to talk to her parents.

"Los Caballeros?" he asked.

"Yes. And without the *Viejos*."

"Understood."

I arrived at the Los Caballeros wine caves just before noon on January first and made my way through the rarely used corridor before entering the secret meeting room.

My brothers were already there—Brix, Cru, Bit, and Snapper. Ridge and his brother, Dalton, had come up from his place on See Canyon Road, Beau and Press Barrett were in town because of last night's auction, and Zin Oliver stood talking to them.

"Isabel Van Orr is missing," Brix said, getting straight to it after everyone took their seat. "Baron has no idea where she is. As far as he knows, she got on a plane to Italy and disappeared."

"He filed a missing persons report with Vader this morning," Zin added. "Sheriff's office is treating it seriously. Baron's daughter, international flight— they're already coordinating with agencies."

"She could be hurt. Or worse. Baron's daughter— someone could have taken her for ransom. Or—"

"Which is why we're here," Cru, seated beside me, interrupted, resting his hand on my arm.

Ridge raised his head. "Dalton, Zin, and I will mobilize PIs here in the States. Check hospitals, police reports. See if there's been any accidents or incidents."

"I'll help," Snapper offered.

"We'll head up the international search," said Press, motioning to Beau and Zin. "First thing we need to find out is if she ever made it out of SLO," he added. "She would've got a connection either through LAX or SFO."

"We keep this contained, reporting through encrypted channels only," said Brix. "If there's nothing else, let's get to work."

I was about to ask what I could do when Brix spoke again. "Kick, you're with us."

"Understood," I said, wondering if he knew something I didn't and that was why the only people not walking out were Avilas.

Rather than stay in the meeting room, Brix led us into one of the tasting areas, where he grabbed glasses and Cru tapped a barrel. "I'm gonna leave this up to you, Rascon," he began after we all had wine. "There's clearly more to your association with Isabel, and we need to know what that is. However, who you confide in is your decision. It can be all or just one of us."

I met the eyes of each of my brothers. The only person who'd mind was Snapper, and after what Isabel did, making sure the Christmas Blessing Wine was able to be finished and released, I doubted he'd care, either. Plus, he already knew the worst of it—that I'd been the one who told her things I never should have.

"We became friends after last year's Wicked Winemakers' Ball. I wasn't around much, as you know, but we kept in touch."

"When did it change?" Snapper asked. My eyes met his, and instead of the animosity I feared I'd see, I witnessed concern.

"The night after this year's ball, but it didn't last long."

"You took her to the airport," prompted Brix.

"The first time we really talked was on Christmas Eve. I tried to clear the air between us, and while the call ended with us being 'reconciled,' for lack of a better way to put it, I sensed she was telling me what I wanted to hear."

"What else happened?" Cru asked.

"I called her again on Christmas, then the morning after. I was about to give up after only reaching voice-mail, but then she picked up." I told them how she'd said she was trying to arrange a ride to the airport and when I offered to take her, she accepted. "We didn't talk much on the drive, and when she said goodbye before entering the terminal, I gotta tell you, it felt like it was forever."

Snapper put his hand on my shoulder. "We're gonna find her, Kick."

"What can I do?"

"You know the drill. The one who comes to the *caballeros* for help steps aside," he responded before his eyes met Snapper's.

"What?" I asked.

"I'm in charge of keeping you out of trouble," said Snapper.

"No," I blurted. "Sorry, but I…can't."

"Then, you're with me," said Bit. "Come on. Let's get out of here."

My eyes met Snapper's once more, and again, instead of anger, they were filled only with concern.

"Sorry," I muttered.

He shook his head. "Bit's more fun than me anyway."

"Damn straight," our older brother muttered as he took my arm and led me out of the room.

"Where are we going?" I asked once we were out of the caves.

"My place, and when we get there, you're gonna concentrate long and hard about what Isabel might have said or done that you didn't pick up on."

"I already did."

"Not my way, you didn't."

My mouth gaped. "What's your way?"

"Hypnosis."

"You're joking."

He shrugged a shoulder. "Maybe. Then again, maybe not."

My brother's so-called "hypnosis" involved us working the dormant fields at his ranch, Poppy Hill, until I was so exhausted I could hardly move. The good news was that, once I got home, I slept so hard I didn't wake up until I got a call from Press a little before noon.

"She flew SLO to San Francisco. Same day you dropped her off. But she never boarded the international connection to Italy. She rented a car at SFO instead."

San Francisco. Not Italy.

"Can you track her after that?"

"Working on it. She paid cash for the rental, but the company has GPS data. Ridge's PIs are on it."

I spent the next twenty-four hours obsessively checking for messages. And trying to reach Isabel. Small updates trickled in—the rental car GPS had been disabled after she left the airport. No hospital admissions matching her description. No police reports. No accidents.

She'd vanished somewhere into Northern California.

Finally, an update came in Sunday morning at seven. "Meeting in the caves as soon as you can get there," Brix said. "We found her."

5

Isabel

It was just after eight in the morning when I had my single suitcase packed and was ready to check out of the rental cottage. Everything I had fit into one bag. The realization should have bothered me more than it did. Even the subcompact rental car should have, but it didn't. This was my life now, and honestly, I kinda liked it. At least I wasn't walking on eggshells every minute of every day, wondering what else I'd do to piss off my father.

Bas had texted me to meet him at the main house at nine. Knowing it would only take ten minutes to get there, at a quarter to, I headed over. When I arrived, he was waiting on the porch, coffee cup in hand, and his easy smile already in place.

"Morning, Izzy!" He jogged down the steps as I parked. "Ready to see your new place?"

"Lead the way."

He opened my car door with an exaggerated bow. "Your chariot awaits. Well, my truck. Close enough."

I grabbed my purse and followed him. The drive around the property showcased their operation—Pinot Noir clones, rootstock choices, and elevation changes that created different microclimates across the estate. His enthusiasm, like so many things about him, was infectious. And he was attractive. Anyone with eyes could see that.

Tall, broad-shouldered, the kind of build that came from years of physical work. Dark hair that always looked a bit tousled, like he'd just run his fingers through it. A face that made women look twice.

If I could fall for someone, Bas would make it easy. But I didn't feel that way about him. I never had. The spark just wasn't there, despite how perfect he looked on paper.

"See that section?" He pointed to rows climbing a hillside. "Best fruit on the whole property."

"You say that about every section."

"Because it's true." He widened his eyes in mock offense.

Three guest cottages sat scattered across the property. He showed me all of them—one near the main house, one by the equipment barns, and one tucked into a hillside overlooking the westernmost vineyard.

"That one," I said, pointing to the last one.

"The farthest from everything?" Bas raised an eyebrow. "Trying to avoid me already, Izzy?"

"Privacy."

"Mmm. Sure. Privacy." He grinned. "Not buying it, but okay."

He didn't push, just drove us there.

The cottage was charming and larger than I'd expected, with windows that overlooked a hillside. It had two bedrooms and a third that was set up as an office. The sole bathroom, which was set up Jack-and-Jill style, had an old claw-foot tub as well as a shower, two sinks, and a water closet.

The kitchen had a gas stove and butcher block counter, and there was a sitting area with a stone fireplace. The furniture was simple—a sofa, two comfortable-looking chairs, and a wooden dining table that sat four.

"I'm sorry. This is more than I need, Bas. You should probably keep it open for someone else."

He shook his head. "They're all the same size, so it's all about location. So this is the one?"

"Sure, and thanks."

He went back out to his truck and returned with several grocery bags.

"Thank you, but you didn't need to do this. I could've picked some things up later."

"Can't have my marketing director starving on her first day," he said as he unloaded coffee, bread, eggs, butter, cheese, fruit, and a bottle of Whitmore wine.

"*Your* marketing director?"

"Dad might have hired you, but you're working with me." He winked. "Lucky you."

I rolled my eyes, but I was smiling.

"He said to tell you to take the rest of the week to settle in. You'll start on Monday."

"No."

He looked up from one of the bags, eyebrows raised. "No?"

"I want to start now. Today."

"Izzy—"

"I need to stay busy. Please."

His teasing faded as concern replaced it. "You really can't sit still, can you?"

"Not right now."

"Okay." He closed the refrigerator. "Get changed. We start the vineyard walk-through in an hour. But you're taking breaks when I tell you to. Deal?"

"Bas—"

"Deal, Izzy?"

Pure Bas. Always had been, since we were kids.

"Deal."

"Good. Wait. I just remembered we need to do something about your rental car. That thing's costing you what, a hundred bucks a day?"

"Around that," I admitted.

"Highway robbery. Come on. I'll show you your new wheels."

He led me to the equipment barn near the main winery building, then past tractors and harvesting equipment to a side area where several vehicles were parked.

Bas gestured to a luxury SUV with a flourish. It was black, pristine, and the exact kind of thing my father would've expected me to drive.

"Ta-da! This beauty is yours. Comes with the position."

My chest tightened as I stared at it. "Bas, no. Absolutely not."

"What's wrong with it?"

"It's an eighty-thousand-dollar car! I don't want any special favors. I want to be hired on the same terms as anyone else."

This was exactly what I'd come here to escape. The pampered life, the luxury, and the assumption that I expected special things just because of my last name. I needed to change. To prove I could make it on my own merit, not on Baron's money or the Van Orr name. I couldn't continue living like his spoiled daughter, accepting handouts and calling it independence.

The vehicle represented everything I was running from.

"Izzy, I'm serious. This is a company car. The marketing director position includes it."

"I don't believe you."

"You calling me a liar?" His brow arched. "That hurts, Izzy. Really hurts."

"Stop it."

"I'm not lying! Our last marketing director drove it. Ask my father if you don't believe me."

I folded my arms and glared at him.

"There are three other company vehicles here." He pointed to a truck and two SUVs. "Want to see the one the vineyard manager drives? The operations director? They all get cars, Izzy. It's standard."

He moved closer. "Look, I get it. You want to prove yourself. You want to earn everything. I respect that. But this?" He gestured to the SUV. "This is just how we do business. Same package anyone in this position would get."

I wanted to argue. Wanted to insist on an older model, a cheaper alternative. But I couldn't without seeming ungrateful.

"Fine. But if I find out you're doing this because—"

"You'll what? Quit? Storm off in a huff?" He smiled. "Come on. I've known you too long for the dramatic exit routine."

"I'm serious, Bas."

"So am I. Now, can we please go turn in your rental before you waste another hundred bucks? That's like… three bottles of good wine. Priorities, Izzy."

I drove the rental car to the return location, Bas following in his truck. When I climbed into the Whitmore SUV afterward, the contrast hit me. Butter-soft leather seats. The latest dashboard technology. Everything about it screamed privilege and wealth—the world I was trying to escape.

My fingers tightened on the steering wheel. It was just a company car. Not special treatment. Just a job perk that anyone in this role would receive. But it felt too nice. Too easy. Too much like my old life.

Back at the cottage, I unpacked my suitcase. Fifteen minutes and I finished. My clothes hung in the small closet, my toiletries lined the bathroom shelf, and my phone stayed off in the bedside drawer.

This was mine. The first place that had ever been truly mine—albeit a perk of the job. The point was, it wasn't a Van Orr property.

I stood at the window, looking out at the rows stretching toward the horizon. No pressure. No expectations. No one watching me, waiting for me to fail or cause another scandal.

The memory of Kick's goodbye at the airport surfaced unbidden. The way he'd looked at me like he knew something was wrong. Maybe he even guessed I didn't plan on returning—ever. On the other hand, maybe he drove away and never looked back. Didn't think about me at all. I pushed the thoughts away and changed into jeans and boots.

An hour later, Bas arrived for our tour. We walked through rows of dormant Pinot Noir while he explained their sustainable practices, soil composition, and yields per acre. I asked questions about clone selection, fermentation processes, and how they balanced innovation with the traditional methods his grandfather had established.

We stopped at a section where the soil shifted from clay to volcanic loam. Bas crouched down, grabbed a handful, and let it crumble through his fingers.

"See how it drains? Perfect for stressing the vines. Makes them work harder, concentrate the flavor."

I knelt beside him, studying the texture. "My grandmother used to say the same thing about—" I stopped myself, throat tightening.

Bas looked at me, his expression softening. "You're thinking about Miremont, aren't you?"

I stiffened. "I don't—"

"Izzy." He waited until I met his eyes. "You don't have to pretend with me. I know what that place meant to you."

"Meant. Past tense." I stood and brushed the dirt from my hands. "It's gone now."

He rose beside me but didn't push. That was Bas—he always seemed to know exactly when to let things go. When to give me space instead of pressing for more.

"You really do know your stuff. Why aren't you working at one of the Van Orr properties?"

"Just because my father never took me seriously—despite the ridiculously expensive education he paid for—it doesn't mean I wasn't paying attention."

His expression changed. "I'm sorry he never valued you, Izzy. You deserve to be, and I promise you, you will be here."

"I know I will, Bas, and I can't tell you how much I appreciate it. But I want it to be because I earned it. Not because you handed it to me."

"I get it. I swear I do." He stopped walking and caught my arm. "It isn't any different for me. My dad didn't give me my job just because I'm his son. I had to work for it, and I'm glad I did."

"How do you always know the exact right thing to say to make me feel better?"

I expected him to make a joke, but he didn't.

"Because I care about you, Izzy. I always have."

Yes, I should've responded, told him I cared about him too, but if I had, it might've given him the wrong impression. Instead, I simply thanked him.

After we were done for the day, I begged off his dinner invitation and made myself scrambled eggs and toast. I took a pass on the wine from the bottle Bas had left on the counter, though. I finished eating, then lit a fire in the stone fireplace and curled up on the sofa.

The quiet pressed against my ears. No staff moving through hallways. No expectations weighing on my shoulders. No father demanding to know what I was doing—or ignoring my existence completely. There was no middle ground with him.

Peace. Space to breathe.

Guilt churned in my stomach anyway. I'd lied to my father, and I'd lied to Kick. Instead of facing whatever consequences were coming, I ran away. I shoved the feeling down. Survival first. Guilt later.

Before dawn the next morning, headlights swept across my window, jolting me from a restless sleep.

I opened the door when I heard footsteps on the porch. "You made me coffee?" I asked Bas when he held out the cup.

"Don't get used to it." But his grin said otherwise. "Ready to meet the crew?"

He drove us to the vineyard office, where workers gathered near a truck—eight men and two women, all dressed in layers against the cold. He introduced me to the vineyard manager first, Carlos, a man in his fifties with sun-weathered skin.

"This is Izzy," Bas said. "She's our new marketing director, but she wants to learn the operation from the ground up."

Carlos held out his hand, and we shook. "Welcome. Have you worked in vineyards before?"

"Some," I responded. "But I have a lot to learn."

One of the women, Maria, smiled. She looked to be in her forties, with dark hair styled in a braid. "Good. We'll teach you."

The crew loaded into trucks, and I climbed in beside Maria. She handed me a pair of pruning shears and thick gloves.

We drove to our first rows and started working. Maria showed me how to identify the canes to keep, which ones to remove, and how to make clean cuts that wouldn't damage the vine. The work was cold and repetitive. My shoulders burned, my palms ached despite the gloves, and my back screamed from bending over vine after vine.

But I didn't stop, and I sure as hell didn't complain. I kept my head down and focused on the work, even as I felt the crew watching me and assessing.

By lunch, blisters had formed under my gloves. Maria noticed when I flexed my fingers.

"Let me see."

I shook my head, but she grabbed my hand. "Let me see."

When I removed the gloves and showed her my palms, she retrieved a first aid kit from the truck.

"You should have said something."

"I'm fine."

"You're stubborn." But she smiled as she wrapped my fingers in bandages. "Good. You'll need that here."

The second day was easier. My body adjusted to the physical demands. I learned to read the vines better, to see which canes would produce the best fruit, and to make decisions faster. I split my time between working alongside the crew and following Bas through management decisions—discussing irrigation timing, reviewing the soil test results, planning the schedules for different sections.

He was patient as a teacher, enthusiastic about every detail.

The crew warmed to me, including me in their conversations during lunch, asking my opinion on things, and listening when I answered.

Maria commented on the third day: "You're not like other marketing directors."

I laughed. "I'm trying not to be."

"And Bas?" She nodded toward where he stood talking to Carlos. "He's good to you?"

"We're friends. Have been since we were kids."

She gave me a knowing look but didn't push.

Over the next few days, I settled into a routine. Mornings in the field, afternoons in my office in the winery building. I dove into sales data, customer demographics, and budget reports—building the foundation for the campaigns I wanted to launch.

For the first time in months, I felt useful. Purposeful.

By the end of the week, calluses had formed on my palms and my muscles had grown stronger. I could keep pace with the crew and make decisions without second-guessing myself.

At the end of every workday, I thanked Bas for his invitation to join him and his father in the main house for dinner, insisting I was too tired. Thankfully, he didn't push even though his disappointment was apparent.

Once alone in the cottage, my thoughts would drift to Kick. I missed his laugh, his easy confidence, and how things were between us. We were friends. Before I ruined it. Before it became something it never should have been.

The crew had a half day on New Year's Eve. I stayed late anyway, working through rows of Chardonnay until Bas found me.

"Come on, Izzy. Even I'm taking the afternoon off."

"I don't have anywhere to be."

"Yes, you do." He plucked the shears from my grasp. "Dinner at the main house. *Thomas* insists. And before you argue—it's not negotiable. Dad's orders. Six o'clock. Don't make me carry you there."

"You wouldn't."

"Try me."

I went because arguing with Bas when he used that tone was pointless.

Thomas' house was filled with family that evening. Three of Bas' four siblings had driven in from their various colleges. Everest, the second oldest, was studying medicine at Stanford. Arlow, the oldest daughter, was in her second year of graduate studies in UC Davis' Viticulture and Enology. The second youngest was Huxley, and he was still an undergrad in the same program as his sister. Brylee, the only other girl, was attending NYU's film school and had been here for Christmas but returned to spend New Year's Eve in the city.

The meal was loud and full of laughter as they all told embarrassing stories about each other as kids. I sat at the table, watching them interact. At first, I felt like an outsider despite knowing them most of my life, but their warmth embraced me. They treated me like family. Not someone to be managed or controlled.

Just Isabel.

As nine o'clock—midnight East Coast time—approached, we gathered in the living room.

Champagne glasses were filled, and we watched the ball descend in Times Square.

Last New Year's Eve, I'd been at a Van Orr gala, champagne in hand, smile plastered on my face, while I counted the minutes until I could leave.

Thomas cleared his throat and looked at me as he spoke. "To fresh starts and new beginnings."

"To family—the one you're born into and the one you choose," Bas added.

My eyes stung, and silently, I said, "To second chances."

I raised my glass with the others, letting it touch my lips without drinking.

A half hour later, Bas drove me to the cottage. The night was cold, clear, and stars filled the sky above us.

"You okay?" he asked as we got out of his truck.

"Yeah. Your family is wonderful. I've missed them."

"And we missed you."

I unlocked the cottage door and was about to thank Bas for a lovely night, but he spoke first.

"You think about him?" he asked. "Whoever he is?"

"Pardon?"

"Come on, Izzy. I've known you since we were kids. There's someone. You get this look."

I didn't answer.

"It's okay. You don't have to tell me. But whoever he is, he's an idiot for letting you go."

"I'm the one who left, Bas."

"Then, maybe you're both idiots."

I laughed despite myself.

"Thanks for everything, Bas." I kissed his cheek.

"Izzy—"

"Good night," I said, ducking inside before he could say more.

I went into the bedroom, dug my phone out of the drawer, plugged it in, and turned it on for the first time since December twenty-sixth.

The screen lit up with notifications.

Baron's messages grew increasingly angry. *Where are you? Call me. You're making a mistake. This is unacceptable.*

Kick left messages, and in each one, he said the same thing. "Call me, Isabel. Please."

I deleted my father's texts without responding, turned the phone off, removed the battery, and set it on the table.

Baron obviously knew I'd never gone to Italy. Which meant he'd be looking for me. But he'd never think to look here, at Thomas Whitmore's estate. Never in a thousand years. Kick probably knew it too.

I went to bed and lay awake, staring at the ceiling, wondering if I'd made the right choice, but knowing it was the only one I could make.

I woke to frost coating the windows. It was New Year's Day—a fresh start.

I made coffee and sat at the small table, watching the sun rise over the hills. The view was breathtaking—golden light spilling across dormant vines, and mist rising from the valley floor.

I left my phone off so Baron's anger couldn't reach me here.

But the guilt could. It sat heavy in my chest, a constant companion.

I pushed it away as best I could and got dressed.

The estate was quiet on the holiday. No crews were working, no trucks carrying wine for distribution moving in and out. Just me, the vines, and the cold morning air.

I grabbed shears from the equipment shed and started working, hoping the physical labor would help quiet my mind. Select. Cut. Remove. The rhythm calmed me.

Hours passed, the sun climbed higher, and the day grew warm.

I worked until my hands ached and my back screamed. Until sweat dampened my shirt despite the cold. Until I was too tired to think about Kick or Baron or the mess I'd left behind.

When I finally stopped, the sun was setting. I'd cleared three full rows.

I walked back to my cottage, muscles trembling with exhaustion. Once inside, I collapsed on the sofa.

My phone sat on the table where I'd left it, battery removed. Silent. Safe.

I stared at it for a long time.

Then I got up, made dinner, and tried not to think about what I'd given up.

The days blurred together after that. Work became my anchor. Mornings in the field, afternoons developing marketing strategies. I threw myself into both with equal intensity.

Thomas called me into his office on January third to review my preliminary marketing plan. I presented my ideas—social media strategy, experiential events, influencer partnerships. Campaigns targeted at millennials who wanted authenticity, not just legacy.

He asked hard questions, and I answered with confidence, backed by research and data.

"This is excellent work, Isabel. I'm pleased."

It was simple praise, but it meant everything to me. The first time in my life someone had valued my work for what it was, not who I was.

Walking back to my office, I passed the crew working in the east section. Miguel waved and called something out in Spanish that made the others laugh. Maria shook her head at him, grinning and motioning for me to join them.

I'd been accepted. As Isabel. As one of them. It should have felt like victory. Instead, it felt hollow.

That evening, I sat at my window with a cup of chamomile tea. The sun set behind the western hills, painting the sky in shades of orange and pink, and my thoughts drifted to Kick. Always to Kick.

What was he doing tonight? Was he at that same bar where we first conversed in something more than small talk? Where our friendship began? Did he wonder why I'd disappeared?

The questions had no answers. And I had no right to ask them.

I'd made my choice. Now, I had to live with it.

On Sunday, January fourth, I woke early despite having the day off.

The cottage felt too small. Too quiet. The walls were pressing in.

I changed into work clothes and walked to the Pinot Noir section. Dawn was just breaking, and the air was cold and sharp in my lungs.

Once I got started, I lost myself in the repetition, letting my mind go blank. No thoughts of Kick. No guilt about Baron. No questions about whether I'd made the right choice.

The sun climbed higher, the frost melted, and my breath no longer formed clouds in the air.

I kept pressing on, vine to vine. This was what I needed—purpose, something to build toward.

Even if I had no idea where I was going.

6

Kick

When I made it to the caves twenty minutes later, everyone was already there. Ridge had his phone out on the table, screen facing up.

He pushed it in my direction as soon as I sat down. "You're never gonna believe this."

A grainy surveillance photo filled the screen—Isabel in work clothes, pruning shears in hand, standing in a vineyard row. Her hair was up in a pony tail. She looked tired. But she was alive.

"Where—"

"Russian River Valley. Whitmore Estate." Ridge swiped to another photo of Isabel talking to someone near an equipment barn. Yet another showed her walking toward a truck loaded with vineyard tools. "My PI was finally able to track her yesterday afternoon. Turns out she's working there."

"She's working there?" It didn't make sense. "Why would she—"

"Because Baron would never look there," Brix said. "And Whitmore's the last person who'd tell him anything."

He was right. Baron and Thomas Whitmore had been closer friends but had a bitter feud five years ago over a property dispute.

I studied the images, trying to wrap my head around what I was seeing. Isabel wasn't kidnapped or hurt. She'd flown to San Francisco, driven to the Russian River Valley, and gotten herself a job at the one winery where her father would never find her. It made me feel like an asshole for even thinking it, but why would Isabel want a job that was the equivalent of a farmhand when she was an heiress to a million-dollar fortune? It was only one of a hundred questions I'd ask as soon as we were face-to-face. And that would sure as hell be later today.

"Vader needs to know," Zin said. "The missing persons report is active. His office is coordinating with multiple agencies."

"Wait." I looked around the table. "Give me until tonight. Let me talk to her first. Find out what's going on. I'll call Baron as soon as I know she's okay. I promise."

"Kick—" Brix started.

"Please. Something's up if she's hiding at Whitmore's. Let me figure out what before we bring Baron and law enforcement down on her."

The room was quiet for several seconds, then Brix nodded. "You've got until tonight. Then we call Vader, whether you've talked to her or not."

I was already standing. "I'm leaving now."

"Kick, wait—" Snapper started.

"No. I need to find out what the hell is going on, and I can't do that over the phone." Mainly because she hadn't taken a single one of my calls, not that I needed or wanted to say that.

I didn't wait for a response. I was already heading for the door.

I threw a bag in my truck minutes after I arrived at home, then got on the highway heading north. Five hours to the Russian River Valley. Five hours to get answers.

The miles disappeared under my tires as rolling hills gave way to flatter land, then more hills. Soon, everywhere I looked were vineyards, bare and skeletal in winter.

The entire way, my mind wouldn't stop spinning questions. Why lie about Italy? Whitmore made sense for the very reason Ridge had said, given Thomas would never contact Baron and her father would never think to look there.

But why hide from Baron at all?

When the GPS announced the Russian River Valley exit, my hands tightened on the steering wheel.

I followed the directions to Whitmore Estate. The property sprawled across acres of hillside, with elegant buildings nestled among the vines. Old money. Established reputation. Everything the Van Orrs had, just in a different valley.

A worker passed by carrying pruning shears as I got out after parking near the main building.

"Excuse me. I'm looking for Isabel Van Orr."

The man stopped. "Who's asking?"

I opened the door of my truck and motioned inside. "I've got a delivery for her." Not that I really did. Other than myself.

"Somebody mentioned she's working in vineyard block seven."

I glanced over at the closest plot marker and saw it was block four. "That way?" I asked.

He nodded once, then went in the opposite direction.

I walked the equivalent of a couple of football fields, not surprised when I didn't run into anyone else, given it was Sunday. At the height of the season, it didn't matter what day of the week it was. In January, when not a whole lot was going on, most of the bigger operations gave their permanent workers the day off.

Gravel crunched under my boots as I walked up a short incline. When I reached the top, I saw her.

Isabel stood about twenty feet away, working on a vine with pruning shears. She wore jeans, boots, and a heavy jacket—no designer labels visible, no diamonds, no carefully styled hair. Just a simple ponytail, dirt on her hands, and the fierce concentration on her work. Even from here, she looked ten years younger.

The polished princess had disappeared. In her place was someone comfortable in work clothes and vineyard mud.

I'd never seen her more beautiful.

Another ten feet, and she raised her head, and for a moment, we stared at each other across rows of vines.

Shock turned into recognition, and color drained from her face so fast I could see it happen. Then the blood rushed back, flooding high on her cheekbones.

She dropped the pruning shears and ran in the opposite direction.

"Isabel!" I broke into a sprint.

She cut through the vine rows toward an equipment barn on the far side of the property faster than I'd anticipated as she weaved between them with the desperation of someone running from more than just a person.

But I was faster. Longer legs and better wind from years of rodeo work gave me the advantage. As I closed the distance, she glanced back, saw me gaining, and pushed harder.

She made it to the equipment barn before I caught her arm and spun her around.

She crashed into my chest. For one terrible, wonderful second, all I felt was relief that she was alive, that I'd found her.

Then she shoved against me. "Let go of me."

I didn't. "Not until you tell me what's going on."

"I lied. I'm obviously not in Italy. You found me. Congratulations. Now, let go."

"Why?"

She wrenched free and put distance between us. "How did you find me?" She sounded panicked. Raw and sharp and undeniable.

"Small world, Isabel." I stepped closer. "Why are you hiding?"

"You can't tell my father where I am."

"Okay, but why?" I asked for the third time.

"He, um, cut me off."

I raised a brow. "He sure didn't let on when he asked me if I knew where you were. He's concerned, Isabel. He filed a missing person's report with Vader."

She looked off in the distance and shook her head. "That isn't worry; it's lack of control."

"Call it what you want, but law enforcement is looking for you, Isabel, and if I can find you, so can they."

She worried the inside of her cheek like I'd seen her do so many times before. It was probably something she didn't even know she did.

I took a step closer, and she took one back. We repeated the dance until her shoulders hit the barn wall and she had nowhere left to go.

"What are you running from?"

"I'm not running—"

"You're terrified. I can see it."

She laughed, but the sound came out broken. "You don't know me as well as you think you do."

"Wrong." I planted a hand on the wall beside her head. "You're not as good an actress as you think you are."

Her eyes met mine. Green and wide and full of things she wasn't saying. Neither of us moved. The air between us felt charged—almost dangerous.

Then footsteps crunched on the gravel behind me.

"Izzy, are you okay?"

I turned when a man approached. He was tall, dark-haired, and familiar, wearing expensive boots that had actually seen work. He studied Isabel with concern, then me with wariness.

Isabel exhaled like she'd been holding her breath. "It's okay, Bas."

Bas. Sebastian Whitmore. Thomas's son. I'd seen him at a few wine industry events over the years.

When I stepped away, he positioned himself between me and Isabel. Not threatening, but the message was direct. "Avila. What are you doing here?"

"Talking to Isabel."

"Does she want you here?" He looked at her, and I caught the way his expression softened. It was protective in a way that made my teeth clench.

An ache I didn't want to acknowledge twisted in my sternum.

"Do you want him escorted off the property?" Bas asked her.

I was about to protest, to puff out my chest like he was, but then I saw Isabel hesitate and waited. I could see the war playing out. Fear, but not of me—that was a relief—mixed with something else. Connection maybe? Neither of us could deny we had one. "He's okay," she responded.

Bas didn't like that answer, but he nodded before looking at me one more time. Then he turned to Isabel. "I'll be close by if you need me. Anything at all, Izzy."

"You hate it when people call you that," I said once he was far enough away not to hear me.

"Only some people."

I raised a brow, but dropped the argument I was about to launch into when she wrapped her arms around herself.

She looked small and vulnerable. Everything she used to hide behind an icy demeanor.

"Why are you here?" The question burst out of her. "You made it very clear what you thought of me. I'm spoiled and—"

"I apologized. More than once, *Izzy*."

I expected her to make some kind of fuss, but she didn't.

"It doesn't matter anymore." She turned away. "You need to go."

"I can't—"

Her eyes filled with tears she blinked away with fierce determination. "Please, Kick. If you ever cared about me at all, just go. Tell my father I'm alive. Tell him I'll come home when I'm ready. But don't tell him where I am."

The plea in her tone shattered something inside of me. "When will you be ready?"

"Maybe never."

"You can't seriously—"

The gaze she leveled at me was the closest she came to looking like the Isabel I'd known most of my life. Proud, defensive, fierce.

I should walk away. Respect her wishes and leave her to whatever she was trying to do. But every instinct I had was screaming that this was very wrong. That whatever had sent her here had nothing to do with her dad.

"Just go. Please."

"No," I said.

She blinked. "What?"

"I'm not leaving. You want to stay here and hide? Fine. But I'm staying too."

"That's insane."

"Probably." I crossed my arms. "But I'm not going back to Paso Robles without getting some answers. And I'm sure as hell not leaving you alone when you look like you haven't slept since I last saw you." I reached for my phone.

"What are you doing?"

"Calling Baron. Not to tell him where you are, but to let him know I'm with you."

"Kick—"

I was already dialing. Baron answered on the first ring.

"Did you find her?"

"Yes. She's safe, and she's with me."

"Where?" His words were sharp. "I'll send someone—"

"She doesn't want to come home yet. She needs time."

A long silence. "*Time*? Is this about the trust fund? Tell her if she thinks running away will change my mind—"

"This isn't about money."

"Everything with Isabel is about money. Or attention." Another pause. "What's she doing? Who's she with?"

"She's working—"

"Working?" His laugh was bitter. "My daughter has never worked a day in her life."

I bit back the response about how he maybe didn't know his daughter as well as he thought. "She's safe. That's what matters."

"What matters is she disappeared without a trace. Do you know how that looks? Jesus, now, I have to call the sheriff and tell him she *needs some time*." His voice hardened. "You tell her she has two weeks to stop this nonsense and come home. After that, I'm cutting her off completely. No trust fund. No credit cards. Nothing."

I glanced at Isabel, who stood close enough to hear her father through the phone, except his words didn't seem to faze her.

"I'll let her know."

I hung up without saying goodbye and looked into her eyes.

"He gave you two weeks," I said softly.

"You told him I was okay. That's what you came to do, so you can leave now."

"I'm not going anywhere. You want to stay here and hide? Fine. But I'm staying too."

"That's insane."

"Probably." I crowded her up against the barn. This time closer than before, so our bodies were a fraction of an inch from touching. "But I'm not going back to Paso Robles without getting some answers. And I'm sure as hell not leaving you alone when you look like you haven't slept since I last saw you."

The way Bas had studied her flashed through my mind. The protectiveness. The intimacy of that nickname. The way he'd positioned himself between us like he had the right.

It—he—was another reason I wouldn't leave. There was unfinished business between Isabel and me, and I'd be damned if I would step aside and let some other guy make a move before the two of us figured our shit out.

She opened her mouth to argue, then closed it. The fight seemed to drain out of her all at once, leaving just exhaustion behind.

She whispered, "You can't stay forever, Kick."

My eyes bored into hers.

"Watch me."

7

Isabel

The thing was, I knew Kick well enough to accept his threat wasn't idle. I had two choices. I could ask Bas to have him escorted off the property like he'd offered, or I could take him to my cottage and try harder to convince him to leave.

"Come with me," I snapped at him, easing around him, then stalking in the direction of the cottage. It was uphill the whole way, and when I walked it alone, I took my time. Halfway there, with Kick on my heels, I was winded. Hopefully, he'd think it was because I was an out-of-shape princess who was suddenly working every day instead of shopping and getting her nails done. All of which was true, but that wasn't the only reason, and before it became more evident, I needed Kick to leave.

"Look," I said, trying to catch my breath once we were inside. "I need this job. You heard Baron. If I don't come home in two weeks, I'll be totally cut off."

He cocked his head. "Why did you tell me you already were?"

I sat down on the sofa. "Because it was inevitable."

"What happened between the two of you?"

One of the things I liked best about the friendship I'd once had with Kick was how easy it was to talk to him about my father. Most people only saw his public persona, not the controlling *sonuvabitch* he actually was. Kick, though, got it. He'd never once argued that "Baron is such a good guy," like everyone else I'd tried to talk to.

Except Bas. Even before our fathers turned from good friends to mortal enemies, he'd picked up on my dad's bad side. It wasn't like he brought it up, but he always seemed to know the right thing to say.

"Isabel?"

I raised my head and realized Kick was waiting for an answer. How could I tell him that there was no way I could do what Baron demanded and not cause our family more embarrassment? I would. That die was already cast.

"What I did…the wine…I embarrassed him."

"You did the right thing in the end. Doesn't that count for something?" He shook his head. "Pretend I didn't say that."

"I can't continue living my life waiting for the other shoe to drop. I'm twenty-seven years old, not seventeen. It's time I stood on my own two feet, and that means not giving in to his threats."

"Has he always been this way?"

I shrugged. "Yes, and no." I wiped away the tear I wished hadn't fallen. "After you hear what I'm about to say, please don't think I'm feeling sorry for myself."

He'd been standing, but sat beside me on the sofa. "Go ahead."

When he put his arm around my shoulders, I leaned into him like it was the most natural thing in the world. "I don't know which is worse. Him acting like I didn't exist, or him dangling his purse strings in front of me like I'm a puppet." I sat up straight. "Which is why I need this job and can't let you being here jeopardize it."

It was as though I could see the wheels in his head turning, and as much as I didn't want him to leave, I needed him to. Not only because of my job, but if I was going to take control of my life from now on, I couldn't transfer my reliance from my father to Kick.

"It's what he does, you know?" I said, sounding harsh, but what choice did I have?

His eyes opened wide. "What do you mean?"

"You're not giving me a choice. I told you I want you to leave, but you refuse to. Why? So you can control me the way my father does?"

"Are you really suggesting I'm like Baron? Jesus, Isabel, that isn't who I am at all."

"Isn't it—" My train of thought was interrupted by the worst cramping I'd ever felt in my life. I grabbed a sofa pillow and held it to my stomach, trying to breathe through the pain.

"Isabel?" Kick gasped. "What's wrong?"

"I must've…eaten something—" Then I felt a rush of warmth between my legs. "No!" I cried, holding the pillow tighter.

Kick sank to his knees in front of me. "What's going on? What can I do?"

"Ambulance," I spit out between clenched teeth.

He got out his phone and dialed. "This is an emergency. We need an ambulance at the Whitmore

Winery." He paused. "That's right. Um, one of the cottages." Another pause. "Symptoms?" he asked me.

"Bleeding," I groaned, knowing without looking.

"Severe abdominal pain and bleeding." He waited a couple of seconds. "Um, I'm not sure." He took a deep breath. "Isabel, she's asking if you could be pregnant."

I squeezed my eyes closed, tears ran down my cheeks, and I slowly nodded. Then, everything went black.

Sounds came in fragments. Sirens. People talking. The jolt of wheels over uneven ground.

"Ma'am, can you hear me? Can you tell me your name?"

I tried to answer, but my tongue felt thick, as though it was disconnected from my brain.

"Isabel." Kick speaking cut through the fog. "Her name is Isabel Van Orr."

"Sir, are you family?"

"I'm the father."

The father. He didn't even know. Not for certain. But he'd claimed it anyway.

Someone was doing something between my legs. Positioning something. I tried to move away.

"It's okay. We're just placing an absorbent pad to monitor the bleeding. Try to stay still," said a woman.

Someone pressed something cold against my arm. A blood pressure cuff. Then a sharp pinch on the back of my hand. I flinched.

"We're starting an IV line. You might be dehydrated."

"Ma'am, how far along are you?" someone else asked.

I couldn't think. I couldn't even remember what day it was. My eyes met Kick's, silently pleading for his help.

"Twelve weeks," he said without batting an eye.

"Any previous pregnancies?"

"No," I managed to say.

"When did the bleeding start?"

"Just now. At the cottage. There was cramping and then—" I couldn't finish.

"Okay, we're almost there. Try to stay calm."

Stay calm. As if that were possible when everything I'd been protecting for the past two weeks might be slipping away.

The ambulance stopped. Doors opened. Bright lights blinded me as they wheeled me through automatic doors that whooshed open. The smell of antiseptic and industrial cleaner hit me, and my stomach turned.

"We've got a twelve-week pregnancy with vaginal bleeding and syncope," one of the EMTs announced as they wheeled me in. "Vitals stable, IV started, moderate bleeding on the pad."

Moderate. Was that good or bad? I couldn't tell from his tone.

People in scrubs appeared and transferred me to a different gurney. Kick stayed at my side, his hand gripping mine.

A nurse looked at him. "You're the father?"

"Yes."

"You can stay with her. Just try to keep out of the way when we need to work."

He nodded and moved to the head of the bed, positioning himself where he could hold my hand without blocking anyone.

The exam room felt cold and sterile. A curtain separated me from whatever chaos existed on the other side.

A nurse helped me out of my blood-stained clothes and into a gown while another checked the pad from the ambulance. Kick turned his head, giving me what privacy he could without leaving.

"Bleeding has slowed a bit. That's encouraging."

I felt another pinch in my arm. "Drawing blood. We need to check your HCG levels, hemoglobin, and blood type."

"Why blood type?"

"Rh factor. If you're Rh-negative and the baby's father is Rh-positive, we may need to give you a shot to prevent complications." She labeled the vials, then looked at Kick. "Do you know your blood type?"

"O-positive."

"Good. That helps."

A woman in a white coat appeared and snapped gloves on. "Isabel, I'm Dr. Cross. I'm going to do a pelvic exam to check your cervix. This will help us understand what's happening." She glanced at Kick. "Some women prefer privacy for this part. Would you like him to step out?"

I looked at Kick. He was already pale, already terrified. Sending him to pace in a hallway wouldn't help either of us. "You can if you want."

He shook his head. "I'm not going anywhere."

"He can stay."

"Okay. Try to relax. Deep breaths."

Kick brushed my hair from my face and brought his mouth close to my ear. "You're doing great," he whispered.

I stared at the ceiling and gripped his fingers while she worked.

The pressure was uncomfortable but brief.

"Cervix is closed." She stripped the gloves off. "That's a very good sign. The pregnancy is still intact."

A breath I didn't know I was holding rushed out of me. Kick's hand tightened on mine.

"We're going to do an ultrasound to check on the baby, and then we'll monitor you for a few hours until the bleeding stabilizes. Your blood work should be back soon."

She asked if we had questions, and when neither of us spoke up, she left. The nurse adjusted my gown and draped a warm blanket over my legs.

Kick hadn't moved. He was so close that his forehead almost touched mine. "Cervix closed is good?"

I shrugged. "I have no idea, to be honest."

"Well, the doctor said it's good. I guess she'd know." He exhaled. "That's, um—" He stopped and swallowed hard. "I'm right here."

I didn't tell him to leave.

The doctor returned a few minutes later and said they might keep me overnight as a precaution. "We'll get you in a more comfortable room, then someone will be in to do an ultrasound. After that, we'll determine if you can go home," she said on her way out.

She wasn't gone five minutes when another woman came in. Unlike the others, she was wearing regular clothes. "I'm with admissions," she began. "I have some questions."

My eyes met Kick's.

"I can help," he offered.

"First, I need identification and an insurance card if you have it."

"I didn't bring—"

"I did," he said, reaching for a bag that sat on the chair behind him. He took out my purse, and I raised my hand to take it, then shook my head. I didn't even have the strength to grab it.

"Can you get it?"

"Of course."

Once I saw he had found my wallet, I let my eyes drift closed.

I hadn't set foot in a church since my mother's funeral, but lying here, I'd pray to anyone who might be listening.

Please. I know I've made a mess of everything. I know I don't deserve anything good. But please don't take this baby from me. He or she is all I have.

I thought about Christmas afternoon and the test I'd taken in the bathroom of my childhood home while my father sat in his study after threatening to cut me off if I brought another scandal to our family. Two pink lines had confirmed it was already too late for me to promise I wouldn't.

I thought about the days since. The exhaustion I'd blamed on stress. The nausea I'd hidden by eating saltines before getting out of bed. The way I'd pressed my hand to my stomach in quiet moments, trying to believe something was actually growing there.

I thought about how I'd imagined telling Kick. Someday. When I'd figured out how to be someone worth loving. When I'd proven I could stand on my own. When I had something to offer besides complications and baggage.

Not like this.

Never like this.

I opened my eyes and realized I must've drifted off when I heard someone say, "We're going to get you moved to a more comfortable room now."

When I looked up at Kick, his eyes were tight. He still held my hand as they wheeled me to an elevator, then all the way to the room.

Finally, when I was settled and we were alone, I asked what was wrong.

"Nothing, other than I'm worried about you."

"I'm sorry I didn't tell you."

He moved a chair closer to the bed so he could hold both of my hands. "I understand, and I'm not just saying that."

Tears filled my eyes. "I know there's something. If you don't want to be here—"

"Shh." He put a finger on my lips, then wiped my tears with the pad of his thumb. "Yes, I have something on my mind, but I am not upset with you. Not in any way."

My eyes darted back and forth between his. In the same way I'd sensed there was something going on, I also knew he wasn't lying to me now.

"Believe me?" he asked.

"I do."

"Good. Now, rest if that's what you need. When you wake up, I'll be in the same place I am now."

He stroked my hair, and I let my eyes drift closed. There'd never been a time in my life when I trusted in anyone the way I did Kick. It was sad to think I couldn't say that about either of my parents.

Rather than allow myself to get lost in what would only lead to more tears, I did as Kick had suggested and slept.

"Ms. Van Orr?" I heard someone say at the same time I felt a hand on my arm. I opened my eyes and looked around the room. Kick wasn't in the chair beside me, but he waved from right outside the door.

"I had to take a call, but I'll be right in," he said.

The ultrasound technician, a woman who looked to be in her fifties, had kind eyes and a calm demeanor. She dimmed the lights and shifted the machine closer to the bed.

"I'm going to do a transvaginal ultrasound since you're still in your first trimester. It'll give us the clearest picture. Is that okay?"

"Of course."

"Is there someone you'd like in here with you?" she asked just as Kick returned and sat in the same chair he'd been in earlier.

"I'm here," he said, taking my hand and brushing my forehead with a kiss.

The technician positioned the wand, and the screen flickered to life with shapes I couldn't interpret.

Unable to look, I watched Kick's face instead. His wide eyes moved across the monitor as silence stretched. Seconds that felt like hours.

Then his expression shifted, and his grip on my hand tightened. And I heard it.

Thump-thump-thump-thump.

It was fast and strong, filling the room like a tiny drumbeat.

"There we go," the technician said. "Strong heartbeat. One hundred fifty-two beats per minute. Right where we want it."

A sob tore out of me before I could stop it. Relief and terror and exhaustion all tangled together until I couldn't tell where one ended and another began.

Kick brought my hand to his lips and pressed a kiss against my knuckles, and when I looked up at him, his eyes were wet.

"The baby looks good," the technician continued, pointing at the screen. "See that flicker? That's the heart. And there's the head, the body. Measuring right on track for thirteen weeks."

I made myself look. On the monitor was a grainy image of something that didn't look human. To think that flutter of movement was a heartbeat—*still there, still fighting.*

"I'll get the doctor to come talk to you," the technician said, handing me a paper towel to clean up. "But from what I can see, baby's doing just fine."

When she left, the room went quiet except for the hum of machines.

Kick still held my hand. He hadn't let go since he walked in. "Thirteen weeks," he said softly. "That means October."

"Yes."

"It's mine."

"Yes."

He nodded slowly and kissed my knuckles a second time. I braced myself for the accusation. The anger. The *why didn't you tell me* that I deserved.

Instead, his thumb traced circles on the back of my hand. "I prayed it was." His eyes closed slowly, and when they opened, his expression had changed. "There's something else we need to talk about, Isabel. I wish it could wait, but it can't."

8

Kick

Before I could tell Isabel about the phone call I'd just taken, the doctor who'd seen her in the triage area walked into the room.

"How are you feeling?" she asked.

"Tired, but otherwise, okay. The pain is gone," Isabel answered.

"I've reviewed your ultrasound, and the good news is your baby looks healthy. The heartbeat is strong, and the measurements are appropriate for your dates."

"Then, why was there bleeding?" I asked.

"It's called a threatened miscarriage. It's more common than people realize, especially in the first trimester." She turned to Isabel. "Have you been under significant stress lately?"

A laugh almost escaped me. *Stress?* Running from her father. Hiding a pregnancy. Starting a new job. Then me showing up and refusing to leave?

"A little," she said so softly I could barely hear her.

"And physical exertion? Your chart says you work in the vineyard?"

"I just started. I've been doing pruning, mostly."

The doctor nodded. "That needs to stop. At least for now. I'm putting you on modified bed rest for at least two weeks. That means no strenuous activity, no lifting anything heavy, no being on your feet for extended periods. Light walking around your home is fine, but that's it."

"But my job—"

"You can request time off from a job, but growing a human being is nonnegotiable." She was firm but not unkind. "Is there someone who can stay with you? You shouldn't be alone, especially for the next few days while we monitor the situation."

Before she could answer, I did. "I'll be with her."

She turned to look at me, and I held her gaze steadily, daring her to argue.

I breathed a sigh of relief when she didn't.

"Good." The doctor made a note in her chart. "I want you to follow up with your OB within the week."

Isabel's brow furrowed, and she worried the inside of her cheek. "I, um, just moved here…"

"Not a problem. We can give you a referral. In the meantime, watch for heavy bleeding—soaking through a pad in an hour—severe cramping, or fever. Any of those, you come straight back to the ER."

"Okay," she and I responded at the same time.

"Given how positive the ultrasound looked, I'll let you go home in an hour as long as you promise to rest, hydrate, and try to minimize stress." She almost smiled at that last one, as if she knew how impossible it sounded. "Your baby is a fighter. Give them the best chance by taking care of yourself."

When she left, the silence returned.

"You said there's something we need to talk about?"

Given the doctor's warning about stress, I hated to bring it up, but she had to know. I stroked the back of her hand. "It's about your insurance."

She closed her eyes. "I don't have any, do I?"

"None that the admissions people could verify. But I don't want you to worry. There's an easy solution, whether short- or long-term."

"I won't go home. I can't."

"I support that one hundred percent."

She studied me. "What did you do?"

I probably shouldn't have smiled, but I did. "Nothing big. I looked over at the clock. They said the chaplain can be here in about an hour."

"The *what*?" she shrieked and yanked her hand from mine.

I chuckled. "I'm kidding." I reached for her hand again, relieved when she didn't resist my taking it. "I signed on as the responsible party."

"Kick, I can't let you do that."

"Isabel?" I kissed the back of her hand again. It was as though I couldn't stop myself. "The baby is mine, right?"

"Yes, but—"

"That means I *am* the responsible party." I winked, hoping she'd smile, and she did.

"My job comes with benefits. I don't know how long it takes, though." She groaned. "I have to tell Thomas, which means I might not have a job much longer anyway."

I didn't know Thomas Whitmore personally, but I doubted very much that he'd fire Isabel because she was pregnant.

The discharge paperwork took forever, which gave me time to arrange for a ride back to Whitmore. Press lived in Napa Valley with his wife, Luisa. The two ran his family's vineyard estate, Barrett Family Vintners. Given the hospital was less than a ten-mile drive, he was waiting at the entrance by the time I wheeled Isabel out the front door.

When she spotted him, she looked up at me. "Does he know?" She gasped.

"He does not. No one will until you and I agree to tell them. Okay?"

"Thank you."

I stopped, rounded the wheelchair, and put one hand on each of its arms. "Isabel, you may not believe me right now, but I intend to prove to you that you can trust me. Your welfare and that of our baby are the most important thing to me."

"Thanks," she repeated just as Press exited his SUV and came around to open the passenger door.

Other than his greeting both of us, the conversation on the drive to Whitmore was minimal. Mostly small talk and absolutely nothing about why Isabel was in the hospital. Exactly as I'd anticipated.

The cottage was dark when we arrived. I helped Isabel inside, flipping on lights as we went.

"When's the last time you ate?" I asked.

"Breakfast? Maybe?"

"That's what I thought." I steered her toward the sofa. "Sit. I'll make something."

"You don't have to—"

"Isabel," I said gently. "Let me do this. Please."

When she sat, I covered her with a blanket that spread across the back, then lit a fire.

Once in the small kitchen, I opened cabinets, looking for a pan, cracked the eggs I found in the refrigerator into a bowl, then cut a few slices of bread that I put in the toaster. For tonight, the meal would suffice. Tomorrow, I'd go shopping to get more of what I knew she liked to eat.

I carried two plates of scrambled eggs and toast over to her and sat down too.

She ate quickly, and when she was finished, I could see the exhaustion hit her like a wall.

"Time to get you into bed," I said, helping her up.

"That way," she said, pointing to the left. "The guest room's the other way, and there are clean sheets in the closet."

I didn't argue or push for more. Had she suggested I leave, it would've been another story. "We'll figure out the rest tomorrow," I said, trying to help her get settled without being intrusive.

"There are sweats and a T-shirt in that drawer," she said, sitting on the edge of the bed and pointing.

I got them out and helped her put them on when she looked at me like she expected me to.

"Tomorrow, I have to tell Thomas."

"Understood. Let me know how I can help."

Rather than make a move toward the bathroom, she grabbed the blankets and crawled under them.

"Okay if I sit here for a few minutes?" I asked, motioning to a chair near the window.

She nodded, and I watched as she rested her hand on her stomach.

"Any pain?" I asked.

"No. I just like to"—her voice trailed off—"talk to her sometimes."

"Her?"

She shrugged. "For now."

Rather than taking a seat, I knelt beside the bed. "Mind if I do?"

Her eyes met mine, then she reached for my hand and rested it on her stomach.

"Hey, baby," I whispered. "I'm your papa. I'm so glad you're okay."

I heard Isabel sniffle and reached up to brush away a tear.

"I'm glad you're okay too, Mama."

Her smile was genuine and warmed my heart, then her expression changed.

"I found out on Christmas," she began. "Three hours after my father delivered an ultimatum, saying if I embarrassed him again, caused a scandal, he was finished with me. That was the only time he spoke to me all day."

"Jesus, Isabel. I'm so sorry. I wish you would've felt like you could talk to me."

"What was I supposed to do? Say, 'surprise, remember that one night, well, now, we're having a baby'?"

"Yes. That's exactly what you were supposed to do."

"I don't want you to feel obligated."

"I feel a lot of things, but obligated isn't one of them."

"No?" She turned to face me. "You showed up at Whitmore because my father was worried. You refused to leave because you feel guilty. And now, you're claiming to be the father and promising to take care of me because that's what a good man does, right? The honorable thing?"

Rather than stay on my knees, I stood, walked around the bed, and lay beside her. I eased my arm under her shoulders and drew her to me.

"I'm going to say this once, and I need you to hear me. I didn't come here because of Baron. I came because, when he told me you never arrived in Italy, I was terrified something had happened to you. I didn't sleep or eat because the thought of you—" I stopped and took a breath. "I'm not here out of obligation. I'm here because there's nowhere else I want to be."

"Would you have wanted to know?" she asked. "If I'd told you about the baby the day you took me to the airport, would you have wanted to be part of this?"

"Yes. I can say that with no hesitation. Not just because of the baby. I spent every minute of that drive trying to figure out how to get you to let me back into your life. That had nothing to do with a baby. It was about you, Isabel. Just you."

Isabel's head was on my shoulder when I woke.

I lay in the unfamiliar bed, not moving for several seconds, breathing in the faint scent of her shampoo, and feeling the rise and fall of her chest against my side.

I was going to be a father—the thought should've terrified me. I'd seen my brothers wrestle with the weight of it when their time came. But lying here, with the woman carrying my child curled against me, I felt something I hadn't expected.

Certainty.

Whatever else I did with my life—whether I made wine or didn't, whether I stayed in Paso Robles or built something new somewhere else—I would be a good father. I knew it the way I knew my own name. The way I knew the difference between a vine that needed water and one that needed time.

And Isabel…

I looked down at her face, softened by sleep. The sharp edges she showed the world were gone. She looked younger. Vulnerable in a way she'd never let herself be while awake.

I wanted to marry her—the realization settled into me without fanfare. Not because of the baby—or not *only* because of the baby. I wanted to wake up like this every morning. I wanted to be the person she trusted enough to fall asleep beside.

But I couldn't tell her that. Not yet. She'd assume it was an obligation. Duty. The *honorable thing*, as she'd said last night with an edgy tone.

So I'd wait. We'd spend time together. Get to know each other again. The way we'd started to before the night we spent together in October. And maybe, if I did this right, she'd fall in love with me the way I was beginning to suspect I'd already fallen for her.

Beginning to suspect. I almost laughed at myself. My feelings for Isabel were tangled up in everything—the baby, the history, the way she'd looked at me in that hospital room like I might actually be someone worth trusting. No one got her like I did. No one even saw her the way I did. That had to count for something. Actually, it should count for everything.

And maybe it wasn't love or even something that could become love, or just the overwhelming reality of everything we were facing together. But I wanted to find out.

She stirred against me, then went still.

"Kick?" Her voice was rough with sleep.

"I'm here."

She lifted her head, blinking. Confusion crossed her face as she took in our position—my arm around her, her body pressed to mine, me still dressed in the clothes from last night.

"We fell asleep," I said. "Both of us. I meant to go to the guest room, but…"

"You stayed."

"I stayed."

Something flickered in her eyes. Not anger. Not the wall she usually put up. "I'm glad you did."

Four words that shouldn't have meant so much, but they did.

"How do you feel?" I asked.

She shifted, pressing a hand to her stomach. "Okay. No pain."

"Good." I made myself release her, sit up, and give her space even though my every instinct wanted her closer. "What do you want to do this morning?"

"I need to tell Thomas that I'm pregnant." She pushed herself up against the pillows.

"I can come with you if you'd like."

"No." She shook her head. "I need to do this alone. He hired me. He deserves to hear it from me without—" She gestured between us. "Without complications."

I wanted to argue. Wanted to be there in case Whitmore reacted badly, in case she needed backup. But this wasn't my call to make.

"Okay," I said. "I'll support whatever you want to do."

The look she gave me was searching, like she was testing whether I meant it. "You don't have to wait around."

"Isabel." I caught her hand. "Where am I gonna go if I don't stay here?"

She shrugged, then smiled. "Is it too early for me to blame stupid questions on being pregnant?"

"I'd take that pass every chance I got if I were you. Does it count for expectant fathers too?"

This time, she laughed as she got out of bed and went through a door I saw led to the bathroom.

After she left, the cottage felt too quiet.

I made coffee with what I found in her kitchen—a French press, beans that smelled expensive—and stood at the window, watching the morning mist burn off the vineyard rows.

My phone sat on the counter. I picked it up, scrolled to Snapper's name, and stopped.

He'd want to know. All my brothers would. But the baby wasn't my news to share—it was Isabel's. Until she gave me permission to tell people, I'd keep my mouth shut. Even with Snapper. Even though keeping something this big from him went against everything the Avilas stood for.

I typed out a text instead. *I'm with Isabel. Baron knows she's safe.*

My phone rang almost immediately with a call from him, but I let it go to voicemail.

He'd have questions I couldn't answer. *Where are you? What's going on?* And I wasn't ready to lie to my brother or explain why I couldn't tell him the truth.

The phone buzzed with an alert. I ignored it.

Twenty minutes later, the front door opened.

Isabel looked…lighter. Some of the tension she'd been carrying had eased from her shoulders.

"Well?" I asked.

"He was kind." She crossed to the kitchen, and I poured her a cup of coffee before remembering. "Actually—"

"I can have one cup." She took it and wrapped her hands around the mug. "He said he'd already suspected *something* was going on. That I'd been off."

"And?"

"He told me to focus on the marketing director position—if I feel up to it. No pressure. No timeline."

"That's good."

"He also said he'd like to meet with you."

I set down my own cup. "Me?"

"He asked if you were planning to stay. I told him I didn't know." Her eyes met mine. "Are you?"

"You know I am." No hesitation. "As long as you'll have me." By that, I meant forever, but I didn't want her to drop her coffee in shock and burn herself.

She looked away, but not before I caught her smile.

"He's in the production building. Between here and the main house." She paused. "He said as soon as possible, if you're willing."

The production building was a long, low structure with corrugated metal siding that had been weathered to a soft gray. Nothing like the Spanish-style architecture of Avila Estate, but solid and functional.

Thomas Whitmore stood at a stainless-steel tank, making notes on a clipboard. He looked up when I entered.

"Kick Avila." He set the clipboard down and extended his hand. "I'm sure we've met in passing a time or two."

His grip was firm, and his gaze direct. He was maybe sixty, with silver hair and the kind of face that had seen too much sun and didn't apologize for it.

"I'm sure you're right," I said. "And, if I may, I'd like to thank you for taking care of Isabel."

His smile was warm. "She takes care of herself. I just gave her a place to do it." He gestured toward a small room in the corner. "Walk with me."

The office was cluttered but organized with stacks of papers, harvest reports, and a whiteboard covered in production schedules. He closed the door and rested against the desk.

"I'll get straight to it. Are you planning to stick around?"

"Yes."

"Even if she tells you to leave?"

"She won't." I held his gaze. "But if she did, I'd find somewhere nearby."

He studied me for several seconds, then his shoulders dropped a fraction of an inch and he uncrossed his arms—small shifts, but I read them clearly enough. I'd passed some kind of test.

"I've been thinking," he said. "Anticipating this conversation, actually. You're an Avila. Your family's been making wine in Paso Robles for generations. You've got knowledge I don't have and connections I can't buy."

"What are you proposing?"

"Consulting work. Think of it as a strategic partnership." He moved around the desk and lifted a folder from one of the stacks. "Whitmore is good, but we could be better. I want to expand our distribution and refine our reserve program. I could use someone who knows this industry from the inside."

I'd come prepared for a protective father figure telling me to stay away from Isabel, not a job offer.

"I'm not looking for charity," I said.

"Good. I'm not offering it." A ghost of a smile crossed his face. "I'm offering work. Fair compensation. And something to keep yourself busy while you're here. After that, all I can tell you is, sleep while you can."

I chuckled. "You speak from experience."

"Five times, in fact. I'd tell you that you sleep more once they're older, but I'd be lying."

"I'm sure my mom would agree."

"So, what do you think?"

"I'm definitely interested," I said. "I'm not sure what I can bring to the table, but I'll help in any way I can."

"Good." He set down the folder and opened the office door. "We'll talk details once you've had a chance to settle in."

The sun was high in the sky when I left the production building. The vineyard stretched out in front of me, winter-bare but well-tended. I'd never worked anywhere other than Los Caballeros, and I was by far the lowest person on the sibling totem pole. It might be nice to have the chance to offer an opinion to someone who would value it in a way I doubted my brothers would.

I was halfway back to the cottage when I passed Bas heading toward the production building. He gave me a short nod—the kind you give a stranger, not someone you'd met the day before—and kept walking.

My phone rang with a call from Tryst before I made it back to the cottage.

I almost let it go to voicemail the way I had Snapper's. But Tryst wouldn't reach out without a reason.

"Hey."

"Kick." His tone was even and unhurried, like it always was. "I heard you found Isabel."

"I did, and I'm sticking around."

"Good." A pause. "Baron's been in touch. He's not happy about being kept in the dark."

"I told him she was safe. That's all he needs to know right now."

"I agree. But he doesn't see it that way." He exhaled slowly. "He's called a meeting. He wants the *caballeros* to find you both."

My stomach dropped. "And?"

"And nothing's been decided yet. But I wanted you to hear it from me first."

9

Isabel

The first night, we'd fallen asleep out of exhaustion. The second night, I had no idea what to expect.

We hadn't talked about the sleeping arrangements. When we decided to go to bed, he'd simply climbed in beside me, and I'd let him. It felt natural. Safe. His hand on my stomach, and his body curved around mine.

Now, two nights later, my fear had faded and my exhaustion had lifted. I lay on my side of the bed—my side, like we'd already established sides—and listened to Kick breathe. He was on his back, one arm flung over his head, close enough that I could feel the warmth radiating off his skin.

I should sleep, but I couldn't. I was too aware of the man lying inches away from me. Very, very aware.

When he shifted and his arm brushed against mine, I held my breath.

"You're not sleeping," he said quietly.

"Apparently, neither are you."

Silence stretched between us. I could hear my own heartbeat, loud in the darkness.

"Is me being here okay?" he asked. "I can sleep in the other room if it isn't."

"No." I answered too quickly. "I mean, yes. I want you here."

His hand found mine under the covers, and he laced our fingers together. Just that. Just holding hands in the dark.

"Good night, Isabel."

"Good night."

I didn't sleep for another hour.

When morning light filtered through the curtains, I woke to find myself wrapped around him.

At some point in the night, I'd rolled toward his warmth. My head rested on his shoulder, my leg was thrown over his, and my hand was curled on his chest. His arm was around me, holding me close even in sleep.

I should have moved. Should have extracted myself before he woke up and this became awkward.

But I didn't.

Instead, I lay listening to his heartbeat, feeling his chest rise and fall. He stirred, and his arm tightened around me reflexively.

"Morning," he mumbled, sounding half asleep.

"Morning."

Neither of us moved. His hand slid up my back, then down again—a slow, lazy stroke that made my skin prickle.

"Did you sleep?" he asked.

"Eventually."

He laughed softly. "Yeah. Me too."

We lay there for another few minutes. I could feel his heart rate picking up, feel the tension building in his body. Feel my own pulse quickening in response.

Then his stomach growled, loud and insistent, and we both laughed.

"Breakfast," he said, pressing a kiss to the top of my head. "Stay in bed. I'll bring it to you."

He slid out from under me, and I immediately missed his warmth.

When Bas first showed me the cottage, it felt too big for me alone. Now that Kick was here, it seemed tiny.

It meant I could hear him everywhere. Making coffee in the kitchen while I lay in bed, listening to the clink of mugs and the gurgle of the pot. Showering in the bathroom while I tried not to picture the water streaming down his back, his chest, and lower. Working at the dining table while I sat on the sofa, close enough that his scent drifted in my direction every time he shifted.

It meant his things were everywhere too. His toothbrush with mine in the holder—blue beside my purple, bristles almost touching. His jacket on the hook by the door. His boots by the entrance, huge next to my flats. His laptop on the table, his papers spread across the surface, and his coffee mug leaving rings on the wood.

It meant learning his sounds, his rhythms. The way he hummed when he was thinking—always off-key, always the same nameless tune. The way he cracked his knuckles when he'd been typing for too long. The way he said my name, soft and warm, like it meant something in his mouth.

By Wednesday, I knew his morning routine by heart. Up before me. Shower. Coffee. Breakfast. Check his phone for messages from his family. Start working on the distribution analysis Thomas had sent over.

By Wednesday, I also knew I was in trouble.

"I've been looking at their club membership numbers," I said that afternoon, desperate for something to focus on besides the way his forearms looked when he rolled up his sleeves. "They're hemorrhaging subscribers."

"How bad?"

"Fifteen-percent drop in the last two years, with nowhere near enough new sign-ups to keep pace."

He set his pen down, crossed to the sofa, and sat down too close, yet not close enough. His thigh pressed against mine through the fabric of my leggings.

"Show me," he said.

I turned the laptop so he could see, hyperaware of his proximity. The warmth of his body. The way he leaned in to look at the screen, his shoulder brushing mine.

"Lack of engagement," I said. "They send a quarterly shipment and a generic newsletter. No events, no exclusive access, no reason to feel special. Compare that to what boutique wineries are doing—virtual tastings with the winemaker, first access to limited releases, members-only dinners."

"So they're competing on price alone."

"Which they can't win. Not against the big producers."

He nodded slowly and studied the screen. "That ties into what I was thinking about the reserve program. They're underselling their best bottles. The 2019 Estate Pinot is better than half the stuff coming out of Burgundy, and they're pricing it thirty percent below comparable wines."

"Scarcity and story," I said. "Limit production, create a wait list, make people feel like they're part of something exclusive."

"Exactly." He turned to look at me, and suddenly, his face was very close. "If you're building emotional investment through content, the wait list becomes aspirational. People aren't just buying wine—they're buying membership."

"And if you combine that with the right distribution partners—"

"You create buzz from multiple directions." His eyes were bright now, animated. "Influencers find you on social media. Sommeliers discover you through distribution. They start talking to each other, and suddenly, Whitmore isn't a legacy winery trying to stay relevant—"

"It's the place everyone wants to be a member of," I finished.

"A rediscovery narrative."

We stared at each other. The air felt charged. His eyes dropped to my mouth, then traveled back up.

"We should write this up," Kick said. "Then present it to Thomas together."

"Together?"

"You have the marketing vision. I have the distribution connections." He paused. "If you want to. I don't want to step on—"

"No. Yes. We should." I was aware I was rambling, aware I was still looking at his mouth. "This makes sense."

He smiled, slow and warm. "We make a good team, Van Orr."

"Don't let it go to your head, Avila."

His smile widened into a grin. He didn't move away. Neither did I.

For several seconds, we just sat there, too close, the tension humming between us.

Then his phone buzzed on the table, and the spell was broken.

That night was worse.

I lay in bed, listening to Kick move around the bathroom. The water running. The brush of teeth. The flush of the toilet. Such mundane sounds, but I was tracking every one of them, my whole body attuned to his presence.

The bathroom door opened. His footsteps crossed the floor. The mattress dipped as he climbed into bed.

"Still awake?" he asked.

"Still awake."

He rolled onto his side, facing me. In the dim light from the moon, I could see his slight smile and the shadow of stubble on his jaw.

"What are you thinking about?"

You. Your hands. The way you looked at me today. The way I wanted you to kiss me.

"Nothing," I said. "Just, um, adjusting."

"To what?"

"This. Living with someone." I paused. "I've never done this before."

"Never?"

"Boarding schools. Then my own apartment at Berkeley. Then back to the mansion, but that was just me and the staff. My father was barely there." I stared at the ceiling. "I didn't realize how quiet my life was until you showed up and made it loud."

"I'm loud?"

"You hum when you think. You talk to yourself when you're reading. You sing in the shower—badly, by the way."

"Wrong. I have a beautiful singing voice." He laughed. "But sorry, I'll try to keep it down."

"I didn't say I minded."

Silence. I could feel him looking at me.

"Isabel," he said softly.

"Yeah?"

"I'm really glad I'm here."

My throat tightened. "Me too."

He reached out and took my hand, lifted it to his lips, and pressed a kiss to my knuckles that made my heart stutter.

"Good night," he said.

"Good night."

He didn't let go of my hand. We fell asleep with our fingers intertwined.

Thursday morning, I woke to an empty bed and the smell of bacon frying.

I padded out to the kitchen to find Kick at the stove, shirtless, wearing only his sweats. His back was to me, and I could see his muscles shift as he worked the spatula.

I stopped in the doorway and stared.

This was unfair. Completely, utterly unfair. How was I supposed to maintain any kind of emotional distance when he looked like that? When he moved like that? When he was standing in my kitchen, making me breakfast but looking sexy as fuck?

"Morning," he said without turning around. "Coffee's ready."

"How did you know I was here?"

"Heard you." He glanced over his shoulder, caught me staring, and smiled. "Like what you see?"

"Put a shirt on."

"Why?" He turned back to the stove. "You've seen me in less."

My face went hot. "That was different."

"How so?"

"We were—that was—" I gave up and poured myself a cup of coffee. "You're impossible."

"You like it."

I did. That was the problem.

After breakfast, he went to shower and I stayed on the sofa, with my laptop, trying to focus on the membership analysis and not to think about him naked in the other room.

The water turned off, the bathroom door opened, and he walked out with a towel around his waist and nothing else.

Water droplets clung to his shoulders and his chest. His hair was dark and wet, pushed back from his face. The towel sat low on his hips, revealing the cut of muscle that disappeared beneath the white cotton.

I couldn't breathe.

"Forgot my clothes," he said, not sounding sorry at all. His eyes held mine as he passed, slow, deliberate.

He knew exactly what he was doing.

But two could play this game.

That afternoon, I changed into a tank top and shorts. Nothing I wouldn't normally wear around the cottage. But I made sure to stretch and lean over my laptop in a way that gave him a view.

His jaw tightened, his eyes darkened, and his pen stopped moving across his notepad.

"Problem?" I asked innocently.

"You're playing with fire, Van Orr."

"I don't know what you mean."

He set his pen down, stood up, and crossed the room in three long strides.

"I mean," he said, standing over me, "that I'm trying very hard to be a gentleman here. But you're making it extremely difficult."

I looked up at him. "Maybe I don't want you to be a gentleman."

Something shifted in his expression. Want. Need. Restraint straining at the edges.

"Isabel, if we do this—"

"I know."

"Once we cross the line, we can't go back."

"I know."

"And you still—"

"Kick." I reached up and grabbed his shirt. "Stop talking."

10

Kick

We kissed. It didn't matter who started it. What mattered was her mouth on mine, hot and hungry, and my hands in her hair, her body arching into me as I pressed her into the sofa cushions.

This wasn't like our night in October. That had been frantic and desperate—two people who'd wanted each other for too long finally breaking. Now, I wanted to take my time. To memorize every sound she made, everything I did that made her breath catch.

"Bedroom," she gasped.

"Are you sure about this, Isabel?"

"I've been sure since you came out wearing that towel."

I laughed against her neck. "That was this morning."

"It's been a very long day."

I scooped her up and carried her into the room we'd been sharing since I arrived, and laid her down on the bed like she was something precious. Because she was.

She looked up at me, uncertain in a way I'd never seen her. The Ice Princess of Paso Robles, the woman who'd attempted to outbid everyone at charity auctions for years without flinching—she was nervous. With me.

"Stop staring," she said. "It's unnerving."

"I can't help it." I stretched out beside her and propped myself up on one elbow. "You're beautiful."

"I'm pregnant."

"You're beautiful and pregnant." My hand came to rest on her stomach, gentle over the small swell there. "This doesn't change that. If anything…"

"If anything, what?"

"You're carrying my baby." The words came out rough. I hadn't expected how much that would affect me—seeing her body change, knowing our child was growing inside her. "Do you have any idea what that does to me?"

"Show me, Kick. Please."

I took my time, pressing kisses on each inch of skin I uncovered—her collarbone, the curve of her breast, her stomach. I lingered there, lips soft against her skin.

"What are you doing?" she asked.

"Telling her to cover her ears."

She laughed, but when I moved lower, she stopped.

I knew her curves from our one night together, but it had been rushed, both of us too desperate to slow down. Now, I could find what made her back arch, what made her say my name like she couldn't get enough.

When I settled between her legs, she came apart. When I added my fingers, she begged for more.

I kissed my way back up to her breasts and stilled. "Is this okay?"

"More than okay. I need you."

When I finally slid inside her, we both groaned. I held still for a moment, pressing my forehead to hers, breathing hard.

"You feel—" I started.

"So do you."

I moved, and she wrapped her legs around me, forcing me deeper. We found our rhythm—slow at first, then faster. Her eyes never left mine, and I couldn't look away.

"Stay with me," I said, because I could feel her starting to spiral, starting to retreat behind her walls even now. "Right here. Your eyes on mine."

She kissed me, pouring everything she couldn't say into it.

When she came the second time, she yelled my name. Not Kick. *Rascon.* I followed moments later.

We lay tangled together afterward, the sweat cooling on our skin. My hand cupped her pussy, resting there possessively.

"That was—" she started.

"Yeah." I pressed a kiss to her shoulder. "It was."

After that, the pretense disappeared.

We stopped pretending we had separate bedrooms. Our days took on a rhythm that felt like something I'd been waiting for my whole life.

I woke every morning with Isabel in my arms. Her back against my chest, my hand on her stomach, and her hair tickling my chin. Sometimes, we'd make slow and lazy love again. Sometimes, we'd just lie there, talking about nothing, her body warm against mine.

I made breakfast while she showered. Eggs, toast, fruit—nothing complicated. But every time I handed her a plate and sat beside her, she looked at me like I'd given her something special. It made me wonder what her mornings had been like before. Were trays delivered by staff trained to be invisible? Food appearing without warmth or conversation? Probably.

That wasn't going to be our life. Not if I had anything to say about it.

We worked side by side in the tiny living room, day after day, fine-tuning the proposal for Thomas.

"What do you think about calling it the 1934 Society?" I asked one afternoon.

"Calling what that?"

"The premium tier. It was the year Thomas's grandfather founded the winery. It lends itself to the storytelling angle."

"I like it." She typed it into the document. "Exclusive without being pretentious."

"Like you."

She threw a pillow at me. I caught it, laughing.

The life we were building was exactly what I wanted. Not just the sex—though it was incredible—but this. A partnership. Someone who challenged me, who thought differently than I did, who made everything better just by being in the room.

I caught myself imagining it sometimes. Years of this. A house full of chaos and noise, the way I'd grown up. Kids running through the vineyard. Isabel's laugh echoing through the halls.

Then I'd shut the thought down, because it was too soon. Because she wasn't there yet. Because pushing her would only make her run.

But the following day, I'd find myself thinking about it all over again.

Friday evening, I made dinner. A real dinner—chicken with an herb sauce, roasted vegetables, and bread I'd picked up from a bakery in town. When Isabel came into the kitchen, I lifted her onto the counter so she could watch me work.

"My dad used to do this," I said, stirring the sauce. "He'd take over the kitchen every Sunday afternoon. My mom would sit with him and watch. He wouldn't let her lift a finger. The rest of us would either help or stay out of the way."

"That sounds nice."

"It was chaos. Seven kids, one kitchen. Someone always got burned or broke something or started a fight over who got to lick the spoon."

"It sounds like good chaos."

"The best kind." I glanced at her. She was looking at her hands, and I wondered if she'd tell me what her life had been like when she was growing up.

"Our house was formal," she said quietly. "And quiet. Even before my mother died. If my father was home, we'd eat in the dining room. Sixteen feet of mahogany between us. Crystal glasses. Cloth napkins. No talking unless he asked a question."

"That sounds…"

"Lonely." The word slipped out, and I could tell she hadn't meant to say it. "It was lonely."

I turned off the burner, crossed to her, spread her legs, and stepped between them. I cupped her face in my hands and rested my forehead against hers.

"It won't be like that for us," I said. "I promise you that. There'll be chaos and noise, and someone will probably break something at least once a week. But there'll be love, too. So much love it'll flow all around us."

Her eyes were bright with unshed tears. "You can't promise that."

"I can promise I'll try. Every single day."

I kissed her, and she kissed me back. Then we ate dinner holding hands across the table.

Beneath it all, Baron's deadline loomed.

The day came and went—two weeks since I'd first shown up at Whitmore—and I watched Isabel check her phone too often, as though she was waiting for a gavel to fall. The official announcement that she'd been cut off.

But nothing came.

"What do you think Baron is up to?" she asked that night, curled against my side on the sofa.

"I have no idea." I stroked her hair, keeping my inflection even. "Although I'm sorry to say I doubt he'll just let it go."

"Never. He doesn't know how. Not that it makes me feel any better."

"It wasn't supposed to. It's supposed to keep you alert." I pressed a kiss to her temple. "But whatever he's planning or doing, you can handle it."

"Can I?"

"You know you can. And if you forget or insecurity creeps in or you feel like you have to give in to something you don't want to, remember that I'm right by your side. I'll help, support your decisions, and be who and whatever you need. And if you want, we can face him together."

She was quiet for a few seconds. I knew she wanted to believe me. I also knew that wanting to believe and actually doing it were far different.

I'd just have to keep showing her.

The morning of her two-week follow-up appointment, I woke before the alarm. I watched Isabel sleep for a few minutes, then couldn't resist and slid my hand down her body as my lips found her shoulder.

She stirred. "We have to leave in an hour."

"Plenty of time."

I was right. Barely.

She was still flushed when we walked into the OB's waiting room. From the look she shot me, she knew I was pleased with myself.

"Behave," she muttered.

"I always behave."

When they called her name, I stood with her. The nurse glanced between us.

"Dad coming back too?"

Dad. It hit me. I was going to be someone's dad.

"Yes," I said, and it felt like a vow.

The appointment was routine until the doctor reached for the ultrasound wand. Isabel flinched when the doctor spread the cold gel on her stomach, and I held my breath as she moved the device, but we only heard static. My heart stopped, and Isabel's hand found mine and squeezed hard.

Then—*thump-thump-thump-thump.*

"The baby's heart rate is perfect," the doctor said. "One fifty-six."

Isabel's hand was crushing mine. When I glanced at her, her eyes were wet, just like mine were.

"You're out of the first-trimester danger zone," the doctor continued. "I'm clearing you for increased activity. But no heavy lifting. Four weeks until your anatomy scan."

In the parking lot, I rested my hand on Isabel's stomach.

"Hear that?" I said softly. "You're doing great in there. Your mama and I are so proud of you."

When I looked up, Isabel was crying. Happy tears, I thought. I hoped.

That afternoon, she found me on the sofa with the pregnancy book. The cartoon one. The one she'd probably assumed I'd bought as a joke.

"What?" I said, catching her staring from the doorway.

"I didn't think you'd actually read it."

"Why not?" I patted the cushion beside her. "I've got a lot to learn. Did you know the baby can hear sounds now? Us talking to her?"

"I did know that."

"So when I talk to her, she can actually hear me."

I grinned and shifted, laying my head in her lap so my face was level with her stomach.

"Hey, baby girl," I said. "It's your papa. I'm reading a book about you. You're the size of an avocado right now, which is wild. You've got fingernails and eyelashes, and you can make a fist. So if you want to punch something in there, go for it."

Isabel's fingers combed through my hair. When I looked up at her, her expression made my chest ache.

"She's going to have the weirdest sense of humor," she said. "Just like you."

"She's going to be perfect. Just like her mom."

The next afternoon, I walked back from my meeting with Thomas. My head was full of distribution numbers and partnership possibilities. I'd filled him in on some of what Isabel and I were preparing, and he said he couldn't wait to hear more about it.

I was already thinking about how soon we'd be ready when I came up the cottage steps and heard people talking inside.

"You have options. You know that, right?" Bas asked.

I stopped on the porch and listened, even though I knew I shouldn't.

"Kick is here because I want him to be," Isabel responded. "If that's what you mean."

A pause. Then Bas spoke again. "Do you…you know, love him?"

My chest tightened as I waited for her answer.

"I'm not sure. But I do know that I want this, Bas. I want to have this baby with him. Our baby. I want to see what we can build from there."

She said she wasn't sure. It shouldn't have stung, but it did. We'd only been together—really together— for a couple of weeks. But it hurt. Because I was sure. I'd been sure for longer than I wanted to admit.

"If he hurts you—" Bas started at the same moment I chose to walk in.

He stopped mid-sentence, and his jaw tightened. "Sebastian."

"Avila." He stood. "Just checking on Izzy."

I crossed to her and kissed her cheek. "Thomas said he's anxious to hear our proposal. As soon as we're ready. I told him as much as we agreed to about the 1934 Society. He can't wait to hear more."

Her face lit up. "That's amazing."

"We make a good team." I held her eyes, willing her to see what I couldn't say yet. *I love you. I'm not going anywhere.*

Bas glanced between us. "I should go. Let me know if you need anything, Izzy."

After he left, I picked her up, carried her to the sofa, and held her on my lap.

"I'm not going to hurt you, Isabel."

She was quiet for a moment. "How much did you hear?"

"All of it."

I kissed her before she could apologize or explain or retreat. Kissed her until she melted against me, until whatever doubt Bas had planted faded away.

That evening, we sat on the cottage porch swing, watching the sun set. I'd been thinking all day about what she'd said about not being sure. It should have scared me off. Instead, it just made me more determined.

"I want what my parents had," I said quietly. "A family. A crazy, chaotic, full-of-love family."

Her eyes bored into mine.

"I know I have to earn your trust," I continued. "But I want you to know what I'm working toward. This isn't casual for me. It never was."

I let her silence sit and didn't push.

"I'm scared," she finally admitted.

I turned her to face me, lifted our joined hands to my mouth, and kissed her knuckles. Then turned it over and kissed her palm.

"Then, let me keep showing you."

I lifted her onto my lap, and she came willingly, settling against my chest as the last of the sunlight faded. We sat in the darkness until the stars came out.

Until her phone buzzed on the armrest where she'd left it.

She glanced at the screen and went rigid.

I didn't need to see the message to have an idea what it said. Tryst had warned me two days ago that he believed Baron was ready to make contact.

She held it up for me to read. *Your father would like to arrange a meeting. He's willing to come to you. Please respond at your earliest convenience.*

"What should I do?" she asked.

I gathered her closer. "Whatever you want. Whatever you decide. I'm with you."

She stared at the phone like it might bite her. Baron's silence had finally broken, and whatever came next, the peaceful bubble we'd built was about to be tested.

I just had to make sure we were strong enough to survive it.

11

Kick

Isabel didn't respond to Baron's message that night, or the next day, or the day after that.

She threw herself into work instead. We had meetings with Thomas about the 1934 Society proposal, spent hours in the vineyard with the crew—albeit on a golf cart—and researching sustainable wine tourism kept her up past midnight. I recognized the pattern because I'd seen it before. When something scared her, she outran it.

I let her run, at least for a few days.

I understood the impulse. Baron's message sat there like a grenade with the pin half pulled. Responding meant dealing with it, and ignoring it meant pretending, for a little while longer, that the outside world couldn't reach us here.

But the outside world never stayed at bay forever.

On the fourth morning, I found her at the kitchen table before dawn with her laptop open. She'd been there for a while—the coffee in her mug had gone cold, and she'd surrounded herself with printouts and sticky notes covered in her neat handwriting.

"You're not sleeping," I said.

"I'm fine."

"That wasn't a question." I dumped her coffee out and replaced it with a fresh one, poured one for myself, then took the chair across from hers. "Talk to me."

She closed the laptop and, for a long stretch, just stared at the steam rising from her mug. The circles under her eyes were darker than I'd realized, and she'd lost weight too—not much, but enough that I noticed the sharper angles of her collarbone above the neckline of the long-sleeve T-shirt she wore.

"I don't know what he wants," she finally said. "That's what's driving me crazy. With Baron, there's always an angle, always a transaction. He doesn't just want to *meet*. He wants something."

"What do you think it is?"

"Control." She wrapped her hands around the mug like she was cold, even though the cottage was warm. "Maybe he wants to see if I've learned my lesson. Maybe he wants to remind me what I'm giving up by staying here. Maybe he wants to parade his disappointment in front of me one more time so I really understand how badly I've failed him."

Her bitterness stunned me.

"Or maybe—" She stopped.

"Maybe what?"

"Maybe he knows about the baby."

The thought had crossed my mind too. Baron had resources, connections, and a network of people who owed him favors or feared his displeasure. If he'd wanted to find out what Isabel was doing at Whitmore, he could have, and he probably already had.

"Would that change anything for you?" I asked. "If he knows?"

"I don't know." She murmured. "That's the problem, Kick. I don't know what I want from him anymore. I used to think if I just did the right thing, said the right thing, proved I was worthy somehow—he'd finally…" She shook her head, leaving the sentence unfinished. "It doesn't matter. It never mattered. Nothing I did was ever enough."

I reached across the table and took her hand.

"What if we went to Paso Robles?" I suggested.

She looked up, startled. "What?"

"A long weekend. You could take some time to think about whether you want to meet with him—and if you do, where. Because him coming here doesn't make sense."

"No." She almost laughed, but there was no humor in it. "Baron Van Orr walking onto Thomas Whitmore's estate would be a disaster. Although I doubt he'd be permitted entry."

"So if you decide to see him, it should be on neutral ground. Or at least somewhere that isn't enemy territory for everyone involved."

Her eyes searched my face. "You want to go home."

"I want you to have options. And yeah—I'd like to see my family, and I do want them to know we're together and we're going to have a baby." I squeezed her hand. "No pressure. Just a visit. We can stay at my place or on the coast. Whatever you need."

I could see her turning it over. The fear of facing what Paso Robles represented was written in the tension around her eyes. It was a place where everyone knew her name and her reputation, where she'd spent years making herself the villain at every charity auction and winery event, where whispers would follow her down every street.

But there was something else too—a flicker of want she was trying to hide. She missed it. Maybe not the town itself, but the landscape, the golden hills, the ocean, and the particular quality of light that only existed in that part of the world.

"When?" she asked.

"We could go this weekend. Leave Friday, come back Monday or Tuesday. Thomas already said you could take the time—I asked him yesterday."

Her eyebrows rose. "You asked him before you asked me?"

"I wanted to make sure it was possible before I offered. Didn't want to get your hopes up if work couldn't spare you."

She held my gaze for several seconds, but her thumb tracing circles on the back of my hand gave me comfort, even if she didn't realize she was doing it.

"Okay. Let's go."

We drove down on Friday afternoon. Five hours on the 101, watching the landscape shift from coastal redwoods to rolling golden hills dotted with oak trees. The February sun was bright but thin, casting long shadows across the road.

I kept the music low and let my mind work through what I needed to do while Isabel slept. This trip wasn't just about giving her space to think. Tryst had called me two days ago, his tone serious in a way that had made me step outside before responding.

"Baron's been making inquiries into Isabel's whereabouts. While, by this point, I don't doubt he knows where she is, my hunch is he's trying to figure out how to get her to come home," he'd said.

"What do you think he'll do?"

"I'm uncertain, but the few times I've spoken with him, he seems increasingly agitated."

"As a father who's used to controlling his daughter through manipulation would be," I'd said under my breath.

"Which is what worries me. What will his frustration lead him to do?"

My uncle's next statement didn't surprise me. I'd anticipated it.

"I sense there's something you're not saying, Rascon."

"You're right, but I need you to understand that, for now, I'm unable to."

"Very well. The family is here, as are the *caballeros*, when you're ready to talk."

It was part of the reason I wanted to go home. To make sure we had their support if Baron did something rash. Given I was a current member of Los Caballeros, as were all of my brothers, and Baron was a *Viejo*—the generation that came before us—discord was unacceptable, and I hated that I might be the person responsible for it.

Isabel stirred as we crossed into San Luis Obispo County. She blinked awake slowly, stretching in her seat, and looked out the window at the familiar hills rolling past.

"Almost there," I said.

"I know." She watched the landscape for a while before speaking again. "I used to love this drive. Before my mom died, we'd go to San Francisco for shopping trips, just the two of us. On the way home, she'd point out all the vineyards and tell me stories about the families who owned them—the feuds, the romances, the drama. She made it sound like a soap opera."

"Good memories?"

"The best ones I have of her." She turned to look at me, her expression softer than usual. "She'd approve of us, I think. She always said I needed someone who wouldn't let me get away with my nonsense."

"Is that what I do? Not let you get away with things?"

"Sometimes." She smiled. "When it matters."

We drove in comfortable silence for a few miles before she asked about my mother. While our community was small, Isabel had always been more of an acquaintance than a family friend.

"She's not easy to describe. Warm, loud, impossible to argue with. She raised the seven of us basically on her own after my dad died, and she did it without ever losing her mind, which is a miracle, honestly." I smiled at the memories flooding in. "She'll probably cry when we tell her about the baby. Fair warning."

"Cry?"

"Happy tears. She's been waiting for me to bring someone home for years." I grinned. "This weekend, all bets are off. She's going to feed you until you can't move, show you my baby pictures, and probably interrogate you about our plans for the future while pretending she's just making conversation."

"That sounds…" She paused.

"Terrifying?"

"I was going to say nice," she said barely above a whisper.

We drove up to the main house just as the sun was starting to sink toward the hills.

I'd barely put the car in park before the front door flew open.

"Mijo!" My mother crossed the distance in seconds, hugging me just as my feet hit the ground. "You're here. Finally."

"Hi, Ma." I wrapped my arms around her, breathing in her familiar scent.

She leaned away, put her hands on my cheeks, and studied me the way she always did when I came home. "You look good. Rested." Her eyes shifted to Isabel, who had come around the car and stood a few feet away, her posture uncertain. "And you brought someone."

"I did." I reached for Isabel's hand, drawing her forward. "Ma, you know Isabel Van Orr. Isabel, this is Lucia."

"We've met at various events over the years. It's lovely to have you here, Isabel. Welcome to our home."

"Thank you for having me, Mrs. Avila."

"Lucia, please." She waved away the formality and embraced Isabel in a way that clearly caught her off guard. "Any friend of Rascon's is welcome here. Come with me, both of you. I have dinner almost ready."

Isabel shot me a startled look over my mom's shoulder. I just smiled.

Inside, the house smelled like garlic and tomatoes and fresh bread, as Ma ushered us into the dining room. "Rascon, get whatever you and Isabel would like to drink."

I went to the kitchen and poured us two tall glasses of ice water.

"Sit, sit," she said, gesturing toward the table when I joined them. "Talk to me. Tell me everything. How long are you staying? What have you been doing with yourselves?"

I let Isabel answer the questions about work while I watched the two of them together. Isabel was nervous—I could see it in the too-straight line of her spine—but by the time dinner was on the table, some of the tension had left her shoulders.

"Ma," I said, once we'd made it through the first course, "there's something I want to tell you."

Her intense gaze settled on me.

"Isabel and I are together. And it's serious." I reached for Isabel's hand on the table. "She's important to me."

My mother's face broke into a smile so wide it crinkled the corners of her eyes. "I knew it. The moment you walked in, I knew." She stood from her chair and came around the table to embrace us both—first me, then Isabel, holding her a beat longer. "Welcome to the family, *mija*."

Isabel's emotion was apparent when she responded. "Thank you."

Ma returned to her seat. "This calls for a celebration. Tomorrow, I'll host a luncheon at the Stonehouse. All the women of the family." She began counting on her fingers. "Saffron, Alex, Jaicon, Addison, Eberly, Ainsley, Daphne. You are the final member to join our family, Isabel. Let us welcome you properly."

Isabel's hand tightened on mine.

"That's very generous," she said, "but you don't have to go to any trouble—"

"Trouble?" Ma laughed. "This is not trouble. This is joy. Besides, I've been looking for an excuse to get everyone together." She reached across and patted Isabel's hand. "Say yes. Let us do this for you."

Isabel looked at me, and I gave her hand a gentle squeeze—in support, not pressure. This was her choice.

"Yes," she said. "Thank you. I'd like that."

"Wonderful." Ma clapped her hands together. "I'll make the calls tonight. Noon tomorrow. The men can entertain themselves."

I hadn't yet figured out how I'd be able to sneak away to meet with Los Caballeros, and this would give me the perfect opportunity. I excused myself a few minutes later and stepped out onto the back porch with my phone. Snapper picked up on the second ring.

"I heard you're headed home," he said.

"Actually, we're already here. Listen, Ma just invited Isabel to lunch tomorrow at the Stonehouse. All the women."

"Good timing. We should schedule the meeting then. Same time, different location."

"That's what I was thinking."

"I'll let everyone know. How is she?"

I looked through the window at Isabel and my mother, still talking at the table. Isabel was smiling at something Ma had said—a real smile. Seeing her here now made me realize how significant her trans-formation was. Her hair hung in loose curls that, until a few weeks ago, I didn't know she had. She wore no makeup except for a little lip gloss, and instead of the fancy clothes she'd always been decked out in, she had on jeans and a sweater.

"I'm telling you, you won't recognize her."

"What's that mean?"

"I'll let you see for yourself. Anyway, she's good. Nervous, but good."

"She'll be fine. Ma's inviting Saffron, right?" he asked.

"Definitely."

"I'll let her know, and she'll stick by Isabel's side. Ease her into the group."

"Thanks, Snap."

"I'm glad you're home. I've been missing my little bro."

"Little? I've got at least two inches on you, *bro*."

"Yeah, whatever. See ya tomorrow."

I ended the call and went back inside. It was good to be home. I hoped Isabel ended up feeling that way too. Not that this trip would be easy on her. I just prayed that the rest of the women in the family were as kind to her as Ma was.

She was quiet on the drive to my place after dinner. Her head was turned toward the window, watching the familiar streets pass by.

"You okay?" I asked.

"Your mother is…" She trailed off, shaking her head. "She just accepted me. No questions, no judgment. She hugged me like I was already family."

"That's who she is."

"It's not who anyone else has ever been. Not with me."

I parked in the driveway and cut the engine, taking in the house I loved but so rarely spent time at. Up until I went to Whitmore, it had been the rodeo that kept me away. I couldn't even imagine returning to that life now.

"There's something I wanted to ask you," I said, shifting to face her. "While we're here, do you want to tell people about the baby?"

She was quiet for a moment. "She already knows, doesn't she?"

"Probably. She's kind of that way." I smiled. "But she won't say anything until we give her the okay. That *isn't* her way."

"You can tell people if you want to."

I brought her hand to my lips. "I'm not telling anyone anything. It's either the two of us together or not at all. And if you want to wait, we'll wait."

"Say we do it. How?"

"Here's what I'm thinking. I'll ask my brothers to come to the Stonehouse before lunch tomorrow. We'll make the announcement together—you and me. Then the guys will leave, and you can have lunch with the women."

"All of them at once?"

"Rip the bandage off."

"Okay. Might as well."

Yeah, I hated how defeated she sounded when, until we left Whitmore, having the baby was something we were both so excited about, but I wouldn't push.

We got out of the car, and I grabbed our bags from the trunk. As she stood, looking out at the view of the night sky from the floor-to-ceiling windows that were one of my favorite things about this house, I came up behind her and wrapped my arms around her waist.

"This is where we made this little one," I said against her ear.

When she stiffened, I knew what she was thinking. The last time we'd been here, I said horrible things to her. I wished so much I could go back in time and relive that morning.

"Kick—" she started.

I turned her in my arms and kissed her before she could finish. Her eyes searched my face.

"Let's make new memories," I said. "Starting tonight."

She smiled then. It was slow and warm, and the tension melted from her shoulders. "New memories."

I led her to the fireplace and knelt to start a fire while she settled onto the thick rug in front of it. The kindling caught quickly, flames licking at the logs, casting dancing shadows across the room.

When I turned to face her, she'd removed her sweater. Underneath, she wore a simple cotton tank top that clung to the new fullness of her breasts.

"Come here," she said.

I went.

We took our time. No urgency, no desperation—just slow, deliberate exploration. I mapped her body with my hands and my mouth, relearning every curve and hollow, paying attention to the ways the pregnancy had changed her even in the last couple of days. She was more sensitive now, gasping at touches that used to make her sigh, arching into my hands with an eagerness that made my heart pound.

"Isabel, I…I…God, the way I feel about you…" I kissed her throat, her collarbone, and the space between her breasts, wishing so much I could utter what I really wanted to say. That I loved her.

She pushed at my shirt and jeans, stripping me bare.

"Show me," she whispered.

So I did.

The fire crackled beside us as I sank into her, as her legs wrapped around me and her fingers dug into my back. We moved together in the flickering light, finding a rhythm that built slowly, steadily, until she shattered around me with a cry that echoed off the high ceilings.

I followed her over the edge moments later, burying my face in her neck, her name on my lips.

After, we lay together on the rug, a blanket covering us, watching the fire burn down to embers.

"New memories," she murmured, her fingers tracing slow circles on my chest.

"The first of many."

She tilted her head to look at me, her eyes soft in the dying firelight. "Kick?"

"Yeah, sweetheart?"

"I'm scared."

"Tell me what of."

"Feeling too much."

"Me too." My lips brushed her forehead. "Wanna know what I think we should do about it?"

"Sure."

"We let it happen. Love is a good thing, Isabel."

"Love?"

I leaned down and kissed her stomach. "We love this baby even though we haven't met her yet."

She nodded. "We do."

"So, I think it's time we allow ourselves to love each other too." I brought my face closer to hers, stared deep into her eyes, and let myself say what was becoming too hard for me to keep inside. "I love you, Isabel."

She didn't say it back but she curled closer, her hand coming to rest over my heart. For now, that was enough. It had to be.

"Rascon?" she whispered a few minutes later.

"Yeah?"

She put her mouth as close as she could to my ear and whispered, "I love you too."

I held her tight, wanting to hear her say it again. Wanting to say it to her again too. But I didn't. The gift she'd given me was so much more than I'd expected. It wasn't *enough*. It was everything.

12

Isabel

The Stonehouse looked like something from a fairy tale. Stone walls rose from gardens that should have been dormant in February, but weren't—not entirely. Pink roses climbed the entrance, their winter blooms stubborn against the cold. Ivy crept across the facade, softening the historic structure with green tendrils. A low stone wall enclosed the courtyard, and through the open French doors, I could see twinkling lights strung across the vaulted ceilings even though it was barely noon.

I stood beside Kick at the entrance, my hand gripping his so hard my knuckles had gone white.

"You okay?" he asked.

"Fine."

I wasn't fine. The building was full of Avilas. Through the doorway, I could see them gathered inside—Kick's brothers, their wives, their children running between adult legs, and Lucia presiding over it all from near a tasting bar with polished shelving behind it. The noise alone was overwhelming. Laughter, overlapping conversations, a toddler's shriek of delight, someone calling out about wineglasses.

This was nothing like the Van Orr household. Nothing like the silent dinners and empty hallways I'd grown up in.

"Hey." Kick turned me to face him, his hands warm on my shoulders. "They're going to welcome you with open arms. You know that, right?"

I managed a nod that fooled neither of us.

"We don't have to do this today. We can wait," he offered.

"No." I straightened my spine. "I'm ready."

Another lie. But I'd been lying to myself for so long that one more barely registered.

Kick pressed a kiss to my forehead, letting his lips linger there for a few seconds. His breath was warm against my skin, and I let myself draw strength from his steadiness.

"I love you," he murmured. "Remember that."

"I love you too."

He took my hand, and we walked inside together.

The room went quiet when we entered.

Not silent—there were too many people for true silence—but the conversations died down as heads turned in our direction. I felt every pair of eyes cataloging my appearance. The loose waves in my hair instead of my usual tight bun. The slight swell of my stomach that I'd stopped trying to hide beneath structured blazers and empire waists.

Lucia reached us first.

"Mijo." She pulled Kick into a hug that looked like it might crack his ribs, then turned to me with that same warm smile from last night. "Isabel. I'm so glad you're here."

Before I could respond, she embraced me too. Her arms were strong and sure, and she smelled like cinnamon and something floral—gardenia, maybe, or jasmine. My throat tightened at the unexpected tenderness.

"Thank you for having me," I managed.

"Having you?" She laughed, a rich sound that filled the space around us. "You're family now. No invitation necessary."

Her words landed in my chest and stayed there, sharp-edged and uncomfortable.

Kick's brothers descended next. I'd met them before at various wine industry events, but usually from a distance. Always as Baron Van Orr's daughter, the woman who made a spectacle of herself at the bachelor auction every year. Now, they shook my hand, clapped Kick on the shoulder, and made jokes about their baby brother finally settling down.

Brix was the quietest of them, his handshake firm but brief. His dark eyes assessed me without revealing his conclusions. Cru was warmer, asking about our work at Whitmore with genuine interest, wanting to know about the reserve program and distribution channels. Bit grinned and told me I must be a saint to put up with Kick, then ducked when his younger brother swung at him.

Tryst, Kick's uncle, held my hand in both of his. "Welcome to the family, Isabel. Kick is lucky to have found you."

"Thank you," I said, and meant it, even as I wondered how long it would take them all to realize their mistake.

The other women hung back at first, watching from near the tasting bar.

Saffron was the first to approach me. She stepped forward and squeezed my hand. "I'm so glad you're here, Isabel. I mean that," she said with a smile that meant more than she probably knew.

"Everyone," Kick called out, clapping his hands to gather attention. "Isabel and I have news we'd like to share."

The room went quiet again. This time, true silence. Even the children stopped moving, as if they sensed the gravity of the moment. A toddler—little Trystan, I remembered, Bit's son—squirmed in Eberly's arms but didn't make a sound.

Kick squeezed my hand. We'd talked about this last night, how we wanted to announce it together, how he'd take the lead if I needed him to. I needed him to.

"Isabel and I are having a baby," he said, looking at me with so much emotion that my heart swelled. "She's my family now. And that means she's yours too."

For three heartbeats, nothing happened.

Then Lucia burst into tears.

"A baby," she whispered, pressing her hands to her chest. "Another grandbaby. Oh, *mijo*."

The room erupted. Congratulations poured in from every direction. Brix shook Kick's hand and smiled at me. Actually smiled. Cru embraced him and pounded his back. Bit whooped loud enough to startle little Trystan into crying, which made everyone laugh.

The women moved toward me in a tide of smiles and questions. Addison reached me first, her red hair catching the light from the twinkling strings overhead.

"When are you due?" she asked.

"July."

"Do you know what you're having?"

"Not yet." If someone else was asking me these same questions, I'd probably bristle. But Addy was one of the nicest people I'd ever met.

"How are you feeling?"

"Fine, mostly. Tired sometimes."

Daphne appeared at my elbow, her smile genuine. "The exhaustion gets better in the second trimester," she said in an Australian accent.

"You'll want ginger tea," Eberly added, bouncing little Trystan on her hip. "I lived on it for months."

The responses seemed to satisfy them. No one asked how Kick and I had gotten together or why we'd kept the pregnancy secret for so long. No one mentioned my history with Snapper or the chaos I'd caused at last year's Wicked Winemakers' Ball. They just accepted the news. Like none of that mattered anymore.

I didn't know what to do with that.

"Wait, wait." Cristobal raised his hand from across the room. He stood beside a woman with auburn hair and kind eyes—Ainsley, I remembered. His wife. "As long as we're sharing news…"

He looked at Ainsley. She looked back at him. An unspoken question passed between them, then her cheeks flushed pink, and she nodded.

"We're pregnant too," Ainsley announced. Her smile was radiant, transforming her whole face. "Due in September."

The room erupted a second time. More tears from Lucia, who seemed incapable of containing her joy. More hugs and congratulations. Cristobal beamed as his brothers surrounded him, their teasing loud and affectionate.

"Two grandbabies in one year," Lucia said, dabbing at her eyes with a tissue that had materialized from somewhere. "Alfonso would be so happy. He loved having a full house."

I watched from the edge of the celebration, my hand resting on my own stomach. Two pregnancies announced in the same moment. Two families about to grow. Ainsley caught my eye across the chaos and raised her glass of water in a small toast. I raised mine back, trying to mirror her easy happiness.

She seemed nice. They all seemed nice.

That was the problem.

The men left twenty minutes later.

"The guys and I won't be far if you need anything." Kick led me over to the French doors while the women started setting up for lunch. Through the glass, I could see the gardens stretching toward a wooded area with bare branches reaching toward a gray sky.

"I don't suppose I could come with you instead?" I said, only half teasing.

He tucked a strand of hair behind my ear, and his fingers lingered at my temple. "You're gonna be fine. More than. I promise."

"Okay."

He kissed me, soft and sweet, his hand cupping my cheek. "You belong here, Isabel. I know you don't believe it yet, but you do. Just give them a chance to show you."

When he left with his brothers and Tryst and the door closed behind them, the room felt bigger without his presence. Emptier.

Saffron appeared at my side before I could take a breath. "You doing okay?"

"Why does everyone keep asking me that?"

"Because you look like you're about to bolt." She said it without judgment, her voice low enough that only I could hear. "I recognize the look. I wore it myself not that long ago."

"How did you stop yourself?"

"I realized that none of them are perfect either."

She had no idea how much that resonated with me. Or maybe she did.

"They don't expect you to be anything other than who you are. That's the weird part. They actually mean it." When she touched my arm, it grounded me. Even if only for that moment.

I surveyed the room, wanting so much to believe her.

But twenty-seven years of learning the opposite was hard to unlearn in an afternoon.

Lucia had taken charge of the food.

Platters covered the tasting bar—finger sandwiches with the crusts cut off, salads bright with winter vegetables, and fresh bread that smelled like it had just come from the oven. Pitchers of lemonade and sparkling water sat alongside carafes of coffee. The children had been corralled into a corner with toys and snacks, supervised by a teenage girl Eberly introduced as a neighbor's daughter.

"Come, sit." Lucia gestured to an oblong table that had been arranged near the fireplace, set with flowers and cloth napkins in deep burgundy. "Eat. You're eating for two now."

I took the seat she indicated, between Saffron and an empty chair that Lucia claimed for herself. The other women filled in around us—Addison across from me, Ainsley beside her, Alex at the head of the table, Daphne, Eberly, and Jaicon completing the circle.

The first few minutes were easy enough. Dishes were passed hand to hand around the table. Plates were filled with more food than I could possibly eat. The conversation resembled small talk—how the weather was already turning warmer, how our drive down from the Russian River Valley was, how beautiful the Stonehouse looked with all the winter roses Eberly had coaxed into blooming.

"I can't take much credit," Eberly demurred when I complimented the gardens. "The bones were already here. I just gave them some attention."

"Don't let her fool you," Alex said from across the table. "This place was a wreck before she got her hands on it. Slated for demolition."

"It just needed someone to see what it could be."

The parallel wasn't lost on me. A ruined building transformed into something beautiful through patience and care. I wondered if they saw me as a similar project—the Van Orr disaster, salvageable with enough effort.

Ainsley shifted closer, her plate untouched in front of her. "Isabel, can I ask you something?"

My shoulders tensed. "Of course."

"What trimester were you in when the morning sickness stopped? I'm still fighting it, and I'm desperate for hope."

The question was so normal, so mundane, that it took me a moment to respond. "Just recently, but it got better gradually."

She groaned. "I wish mine was."

"Small meals help," Alex offered. "I basically grazed for three months straight." She smiled at Lucia. "Despite Ma's best effort to get me to eat my weight in food on a daily basis."

"Crackers before I got out of bed helped," Addison added. "That was my lifesaver with Reagan."

The conversation stayed firmly in pregnancy territory—cravings and aversions, nursery plans, the best prenatal vitamins. Ainsley and I became the center of attention, two women at different stages of the same journey.

"Have you thought about names?" Ainsley asked me.

"Not really. It still feels…" I searched for how to best explain. "Unreal, I guess. Like it's happening to someone else."

"I feel that way too." Her hand drifted to her stomach.

"Have you felt the baby move yet?" Lucia asked, her dark eyes bright with interest.

"A little. Flutters, mostly. She is usually most active when I'm trying to sleep." I half laughed.

"She?" Alex raised a brow.

"We don't know for sure. I just kind of felt like it is." I shrugged. "That probably sounds silly."

Alex shook her head. "Not silly at all. I knew with both of mine. Maddox didn't believe me the first time around, but when I was adamant our second baby was a boy—the minute I took the test, by the way—he went along with it."

"Kick's convinced it's a girl too. He, um, talks to her."

"Alfonso was the same way," Lucia said softly. "He knew. With every single one of my pregnancies, he knew. He was never wrong."

The table went quiet for several seconds, honoring the memory of the man who had shaped this family. I hadn't known Alfonso Avila—he'd died years ago when I was a child—but his presence lingered in this room, in the way his wife and children spoke of him.

"Tell me about him," I heard myself say. "Alfonso. What was he like?"

Lucia's face transformed. The grief was still there, would probably always be there, but it shared space with something luminous.

"He was stubborn," she said. "Hardheaded as a mule when he thought he was right. Which was most of the time." The other women laughed knowingly. "But he loved with his whole heart. His children, his vines, me. He never did anything halfway."

"Kick is like that," I said softly, immediately wishing I hadn't shared so much.

"Yes." Lucia reached across and covered my hand with hers. "He is. More than any of my other children, Kick has his father's heart."

My throat constricted at the simple touch, at the warmth flowing from her palm into mine.

Lunch stretched on.

The conversation flowed around me like water, and I let myself be carried by it. The women talked about their children, their work, and their husbands. They shared stories about Kick as a child—how he'd followed Snapper everywhere, copying his older brother's walk and way of talking until they were nearly indistinguishable. How his first "official" rodeo event was mutton busting, and how he'd ended up face-first in the mud. How he'd cried for a week when his first dog died, sleeping in the barn with the other animals because he didn't want them to feel lonely.

They included me without making a production of it. Someone would mention a family tradition, and Alex would pause to explain it for my benefit. Lucia would reference an inside joke, then backtrack to give me context. Every time I felt lost in the current of their shared history, someone threw me a lifeline.

It was kind. Thoughtful. Deliberate.

And I hated how much I didn't trust it.

"The bachelor auction is coming up in a few months," Alex said during a lull in conversation. "We're always looking for volunteers to help with planning."

I stiffened, waiting for a dig. The reminder of my years of embarrassing behavior.

It didn't come.

"No pressure," Alex continued, her tone neutral. "But if you're interested, we could use someone with marketing experience. Kick mentioned you're doing incredible work at Whitmore."

"I—yes. Maybe. I'd like that."

She smiled, and it seemed genuine. "Great. I'll send you the details."

Saffron caught my eye from across the table and gave me an encouraging nod. I tried to return it, but my face felt frozen.

Little Coco wandered over a few minutes later, her dark eyes curious beneath a fringe of bangs that needed trimming. She was seven, I remembered—Alex and Maddox's daughter. The one Lucia said reminded her of herself. Precocious and inquisitive, with a gap-toothed smile that made my chest ache.

"Are you Uncle Kick's girlfriend?" she asked, climbing uninvited into the empty chair on my other side.

"Coco," Alex warned from down the table. "Don't bother Isabel."

"She's not bothering me." I turned to face the little girl, grateful for the interruption despite myself. Children were easier than adults. They said what they meant without hidden agendas. "And yes, I am Uncle Kick's girlfriend."

"Are you going to marry him?"

"Coco!" Alex stood, but I waved her off.

"It's okay." I managed a smile that felt almost natural. "We haven't talked about that yet."

"But you're having a baby." The little girl's brow furrowed with the serious logic of childhood. "Mommy and Daddy got married before they had me. That's how it's supposed to work."

"Sometimes things happen in a different order," I said. "That doesn't mean they're wrong. Just different."

"My teacher says different is good. It makes the world interesting."

"Your teacher sounds smart."

Coco beamed at the compliment. Then her expression turned thoughtful, and she crept closer as if sharing a secret.

"Do you love Uncle Kick?"

The question was so simple. So direct. No adult would have asked it—not this early, not with everyone listening.

"Yes," I heard myself say. "I love him very much."

Coco's whole face lit up. "Then, you'll definitely get married. And you'll live here forever, and your baby will be my cousin, and she'll play with me, and we'll all be one big family. That's what Grandma says. Family is forever."

The chair felt unsteady beneath me. The walls seemed to press closer.

"Coco, sweetheart, why don't you go check on your brother?" Alex stood and crossed to us, scooping up her daughter with the ease of long practice. "I think Alfonso needs help with his puzzle."

Coco protested but allowed herself to be carried away. Alex shot me an apologetic look over her shoulder. I tried to return it, but my face had gone numb.

One big family. Forever.

What she'd said echoed in my skull like a warning bell.

Saffron rested her hand on my arm. "You okay?"

I nodded because I didn't trust myself to speak.

After lunch, we moved to the comfortable chairs arranged near the fireplace, where the flames cast dancing shadows across the stone walls. The twinkling lights overhead seemed softer now, less festive and more intimate. The children had gone outside to run off their energy, but their laughter drifted in through the French doors.

Lucia settled into the chair beside mine, close enough that our knees almost touched.

"You're quiet," she observed. "Are you feeling all right?"

"I'm fine. Just…taking it all in."

"It's a lot, I know. This family." She gestured around the room at the women whose conversations branched and merged like streams. "When I married Alfonso, I only had one sister. My twin. Our house was quiet. Our whole life was. Even though he only had one brother, Tryst, the rest of their family was so big, so loud. I didn't know how I'd ever fit in."

"What did you do?"

"I stopped trying to fit in." Her dark eyes crinkled with her smile, deepening the lines carved into her face by grief and joy over the years. "I decided to just be myself, and if they didn't like me, too bad. It was the hardest thing I've ever done. But they already loved me. Just like Alfonso assured me they would."

My throat constricted. "How did you know it was real?" I said barely above a whisper.

"I didn't. Not at first." She turned her hand over and laced her fingers through mine. Her grip was warm and steady, her skin soft but strong. "But Alfonso kept showing me. Every day, in small ways and big ones. And eventually, I believed him."

She squeezed my hand.

"When an Avila man loves, he loves with everything he has. Rascon won't let you down, *mija*."

Mija.

My daughter.

Calling me that was like a key turning in a lock I hadn't known existed.

My mother had called me Isabel, always Isabel, in that cool, distant way that kept everyone at arm's length. Even in her final months, when the cancer had stripped away her beauty and her strength, she'd maintained that distance. I'd sat beside her hospital bed and held her hand, and she'd looked at me like I was a stranger she was too polite to dismiss.

And my father—he'd never had a pet name for me, either. Nothing that suggested warmth or belonging or love. I was Isabel when he was pleased with me, which was rare, and I was "my daughter" when he spoke of me to others, as if ownership absolved him of affection.

"I can see it, you know." Lucia was gentle, pulling me back from the dark place my thoughts had wandered. "The fear. You're waiting for something bad to happen. For someone to say the wrong thing, or look at you wrong, or remind you that you don't belong here."

I couldn't breathe.

"But that's not going to happen, Isabel. Not in this family. We don't work that way." Her eyes shined with fierce tenderness. "You're carrying my grandchild. You've captured my youngest son's heart. That makes you mine too. Do you understand? You're mine now. You're ours."

Something cracked inside my chest.

The pressure that had been building all afternoon— through the announcement and the congratulations, through lunch and the stories and Coco's innocent questions—all of it crashed through me at once. A wave I couldn't outrun.

I stood up so fast my chair scraped against the stone floor.

"Isabel?" Lucia's face creased with concern. "What's wrong?"

Everything. Nothing. I couldn't describe the panic clawing up my throat, for the grief and longing and terror tangled together until I couldn't tell them apart.

"I need air. I'm sorry. I just—I need—"

I didn't finish the sentence.

I ran.

The Stonehouse door banged shut behind me, but I didn't slow down.

My feet carried me across the garden path, past the winter roses and the ivy-covered walls, toward the parking area where the trucks and cars waited. I didn't think about where I was going. I didn't think about anything except the desperate need to escape, to get away from all that warmth before it suffocated me.

Kick's truck was where he'd left it, parked with the other family vehicles. The keys still sat on the center console, where he'd left them.

I climbed inside and slammed the door.

For a moment, I just sat there. My hands were shaking so hard I couldn't grip the steering wheel. My breath came in ragged gasps that sounded like sobs.

Because they were sobs. The tears had started without my permission, and I couldn't make them stop.

You're mine now. You're ours.

Lucia's words chased me, refusing to let go.

I didn't know how to be someone's. I didn't know how to belong to a family that hugged instead of negotiated, that welcomed instead of weighed and measured. I'd spent twenty-seven years trying to earn love from a man incapable of giving it, and now, this woman— this stranger who should have been suspicious of me, who had every reason to question my motives and my past—was offering it freely, *unconditionally.*

She was everything my mother should have been. Everything I'd spent my whole life aching for without knowing how to name it.

And I couldn't bear it.

The engine turned over on the first try. I put the truck in gear and drove out of the parking area, navigating by instinct toward the main road. The gate opened when I got close as if I could come and go as I pleased. As if I belonged here. As if I was part of the family.

Except I wasn't. And no amount of kindness could change the fundamental truth that I didn't know how to accept what they were offering.

The tears blurred my vision as the Los Caballeros estate disappeared in the rearview mirror. I wiped at them with the back of my hand, trying to see the road, trying to breathe through the pressure crushing my chest.

I'd done it again. The one thing I swore I wouldn't do. The pattern I'd been trying so hard to break.

I'd run.

And this time, I had no idea if I could find my way back.

13

Kick

I arrived at the caves just as the last of the *caballeros* were taking their seats. Everyone was in attendance except Baron.

Rather than Brix, who usually led our meetings when he was in town, Tryst stood at the head of the long table, his expression grave. When I slid into the empty chair beside Snapper, my uncle gave me a short nod and began.

"Baron Van Orr requested a formal meeting with Los Caballeros three days ago," he said. "He wanted the brotherhood to help him locate Isabel."

My jaw tightened. I'd known Baron wouldn't let this go, but using the *caballeros* to hunt down his own daughter felt like a new low.

"We voted at the end of that meeting," Tryst continued. "Given that Isabel is safe, that she's with Kick, and that she's an adult capable of making her own decisions, we declined to assist."

Snapper shifted in his seat beside me. "How'd he take that?"

"About as well as you'd expect." Tryst's mouth formed a grim line. "He left furious."

"Do you know if he's made any moves since then?" Brix asked.

"None that we've been able to track." Tryst folded his arms across his chest. "But Baron is a patient man when he wants to be. Just because he hasn't done anything yet doesn't mean he won't."

"What do you think I should do?" I asked.

Tryst's gaze met mine. "That's up to Isabel. She's the one who has to decide what kind of relationship she wants with her father, if any." He paused, and in the dim light, I could see the concern etched into his face. "But I'd advise vigilance. Baron is a man accustomed to getting what he wants. When that doesn't happen, he tends to find other ways."

"Other ways, meaning what?"

"I can't say for certain. That's what concerns me. We can't predict what he'll do when he feels cornered."

My fingers drummed against the worn wood of the table as I absorbed Tryst's prediction. Baron had money, influence, and connections that stretched across the wine industry and beyond. If he wanted to make Isabel's life difficult, he had plenty of options.

"For now," Tryst said, "focus on her. On the baby. On building your life together. We'll keep our ears open, and if Van Orr makes any moves, you'll know about it."

The meeting ended shortly after. My brothers offered their support as we filed out of the caves—Brix with a firm handshake and a look that said he had my back, Cru with a promise to check in later, Bit with a joke about Isabel being too good for me that almost made me smile.

Snapper hung back as the others headed toward their vehicles. "You okay?"

"Yeah." I ran a hand through my hair. "I want to get back to her to tell her what happened, but I don't want to interrupt the lunch."

"Then, walk with me. How long has it been since we've hung out in the vines together?"

I raised a brow.

Snapper shrugged. "Just trying to kill some time, bro. But remember this about Isabel. She's tough, Kick. Tougher than people give her credit for."

"I know."

After spending a couple of hours reminiscing about our childhood, our days on the rodeo circuit, and all the stupid shit we did together, we walked to the Stonehouse, where the women's lunch was still going on. I pictured Isabel inside, surrounded by my mother and sisters-in-law, maybe starting to relax, maybe even enjoying herself.

But when we reached the garden entrance, Alex met us at the door, and her expression sent a spike of dread through me. Especially when I walked in and didn't see Isabel.

"Where is she?" I asked.

"She left. We thought she might be with you." Alex glanced back toward the interior of the Stonehouse.

"When?"

"About an hour ago. She said she needed some air. We expected her to come back in, but when she didn't,

Daphne went looking for her and said your truck was gone—which is why we thought maybe you took her home."

The warmth in my chest turned to ice. "It should be where I left it." I pushed past Alex into the Stonehouse. The twinkling lights overhead seemed garish now, mocking. My mother sat near the fireplace, her dark eyes filled with worry. The other women were gathered around her, their conversations muted. The room that had felt so festive this morning now felt heavy with concern.

"What happened?" I demanded.

"She was doing fine," Ma said. "We were talking, getting to know her. Sharing stories. And then…" She shook her head and twisted her hands in her lap. "Something I said upset her. I called her *mija*, told her she was ours now. Her expression changed, and before any of us realized what was happening, she was gone."

What my mother said should have made Isabel feel welcome, but instead, had sent her running.

I took out my phone and called her number. It went straight to voicemail.

I tried twice more with the same result. "Isabel, it's me. Please call me back. I'm not upset. I just need to know you're okay." I paused, struggling for what else to say. "Please."

Snapper appeared at my elbow. "What's going on?"

"Isabel left. According to Ma, she was upset."

"Where'd she go?" he asked.

"I don't know." But even as I said it, a dark thought settled in my gut. "Home?"

"You think she went to see her father?"

"I think she was overwhelmed and scared, and when Isabel gets scared, she runs to what's familiar. Even if familiar is the last place where she should be."

"Then, let's go find out." Snapper dug his keys out of his pocket. "I'll drive."

"Good, because she took my truck."

As we ate up the miles between Los Caballeros and Baron's property, I stared out the window, my phone clutched in my hand, willing it to ring. The silence from Isabel was its own kind of torture.

"You want to talk about it?" Snapper asked after several minutes.

"Talk about what?"

"Whatever's going on in your head right now. You look like you're about to crack a tooth from clenching your jaw."

I forced my muscles to relax. "I'm fine."

"You're not fine. And that's okay." He glanced at me, then back at the road. "This is Isabel we're talking about. The woman carrying your child. If you really were fine, I'd be worried about you."

He was right. I was terrified in a way I'd never experienced before—not during any rodeo, not during any of the stupid risks I'd taken in my twenties, not even when Dad died and the world fell apart.

"I love her," I said. "I know that sounds crazy, given everything that's happened. But I do, Snap. I loved her before I even knew about the baby."

Snapper nodded. "I know."

"You know?"

"I've got eyes, little brother. The way you looked at her at the Stonehouse this morning—that wasn't from obligation. That wasn't a man doing the right thing because he knocked someone up." He kept his gaze on the road, his hands steady on the wheel. "That was a man in love."

I swallowed hard. "She loves me too. She told me so last night. She whispered it like she was afraid to say it out loud."

"Then, hold onto that."

"She's spent her whole life being told she's not worth loving. Her own father made her feel like a burden, a disappointment, and a scandal waiting to happen. Twenty-seven years of that, Snap. How do I compete with that kind of damage?" I turned to look at my brother, needing him to understand.

"You don't compete with it. You outlast it." Snapper sounded so certain. "You show up every day. You stay when she pushes you away. You keep proving that you're not going anywhere until she finally believes it."

"And if she never does?"

"She will." He glanced at me again. "Because you're an Avila. We don't give up on the people we love. Ever. Dad taught us that. Ma reinforced it every single day after he was gone. It's in our blood."

The Van Orr estate sprawled across the hills east of Paso Robles, all manicured vineyards and Spanish colonial architecture. I'd been here a few times before. The place had felt unwelcoming then. It felt sterile now.

The gates of the estate stood open when we arrived, as though Baron had anticipated our arrival. Snapper drove the truck through, and after he parked, a member of the household staff met us at the front entrance.

"I need to see Baron," I said.

"Mr. Van Orr is in his study. He said to show you in when you arrived."

Baron had been expecting me? That didn't bode well.

Snapper caught my arm before I went in. "You want me to come with you?"

"Wait here. This is something I need to handle myself."

He nodded, though I could see he didn't like it. "I'll be right here if you need me."

The guy who'd answered the door led me through hallways lined with artwork—oil paintings in gilded frames, sculptures on marble pedestals, the kind of wealth designed to intimidate. My boots echoed on the polished floors.

Baron's study occupied a corner of the house, with floor-to-ceiling windows overlooking the vineyards. Leather-bound books lined the walls, and a crystal decanter of amber liquid rested on a sideboard. The man himself sat behind a massive mahogany desk, papers spread before him as if I'd interrupted important work.

He didn't stand when I entered. Nor did he offer me a seat.

"Avila." His demeanor was cool, his eyes assessing. "I wondered how long it would take you to show up."

"Where's Isabel?"

Baron's brow rose a fraction. "I was hoping you could tell me. She's been with you for weeks, hasn't she?"

"She's not here?"

"Why would she be?" He rested against his chair, steepling his fingers. "My daughter made it quite clear she wanted nothing to do with me. She ran away rather than face the consequences of her actions. And now, apparently, she's done the same to you."

The statement meant to wound, and it did. But I held my ground. "I know she came here."

"You're wrong." Baron's composure didn't waver. "Isabel is prone to rash decisions and incapable of following through. Whatever fantasy you've constructed about her is just that—a fantasy."

"You don't know her at all."

"I've known her, her entire life." He rose from his chair and moved to the sideboard, his movements deliberate and unhurried. He poured himself two fingers of whiskey without offering me any, then turned to face me, glass in hand. "I've watched her sabotage every opportunity, every relationship, and every chance at happiness." He took a sip and studied me. "And now, she's pregnant. With your child, I assume."

I went still. "I expected you'd find out."

"Did you think you could keep it a secret?" His smile held no warmth. "The question is, what do you intend to do about it?"

"What do I intend to do?" I stepped closer to his desk, my hands curling into fists at my sides. "I intend to raise my child with the woman I love. I intend to give that baby everything Isabel never had—stability, acceptance, and a father who loves her."

Baron set his glass down with a soft click against the polished wood. "Romantic but ridiculously naive." He moved around the desk, closing the distance between us until I could smell the whiskey on his breath. His eyes were hard and assessing. "Isabel is not even able to take care of herself. She's fragile and overreacts—"

"She's none of those things. You just never bothered to get to know her."

"I know her better than anyone. I always have," he snapped, and for the first time, I saw something crack in his composure. "Like every other time she's needed saving, it's up to me to do it. She's incapable of raising a child. You know it. I know it. The best thing for everyone would be for that child to be raised by people actually equipped to handle the responsibility."

My vision narrowed, and for a moment, the only thing I could see was Baron's smug, dismissive face. My hands shook with the effort of keeping them at my sides.

"You want her to give up our baby."

"I want what's best for everyone involved. Including the child."

"You don't get to decide what's best." My voice shook with the effort of keeping it level. "You lost that right a long time ago. Isabel is going to be an incredible mother. And I'm going to be there every step of the way. You don't get a say in this. You spent her entire life making her feel worthless."

I turned and strode toward the door.

"She's not here now," Baron called after me. "But when she realizes what a mistake she's made, she'll come back. She always does."

I didn't respond. I was already tearing through the hallways, checking rooms, calling Isabel's name. The staff watched with wide eyes as I searched the first floor, then the second. I checked the guest rooms with their perfectly made beds and untouched surfaces, the library with its walls of leather-bound books, the sunroom with its wicker furniture and potted palms, and the kitchen with its gleaming appliances. Every door I opened revealed the same thing—expensive emptiness.

Isabel wasn't here. Baron had been telling the truth about that much, at least.

Back outside, I stood beside Snapper's truck, my chest heaving and my hands still shaking.

"She's not here," I said.

"I figured." Snapper studied my face. "What happened?"

"Baron knows about the baby. He thinks Isabel should give it up for adoption." The words tasted like poison. "He said she's not fit to raise a child."

Snapper's expression darkened. "That *sonuvabitch*."

"I searched the whole house. He didn't try to stop me." I took out my phone and called Bas. He picked up on the second ring.

"Kick. What's going on?"

"Have you heard from Isabel?"

"Not since before you two left for Paso Robles. What's wrong?"

"She's gone. I thought she might've come home, but I'm here, and there's no sign of her."

"I don't know what to say." He paused. "But whatever I can do, I will."

"I appreciate it. I'll update you when I know more. Hey, maybe try to call her. If she picks up, ask her to call me as soon as she can."

"Will do, Kick."

I hung up and stared at the phone in my hand. No missed calls. No texts. No sign that Isabel was anywhere at all.

"While you were talking to Baron, I asked Bit to check with Vader about any accidents. There haven't been any."

"That's good, at least. But if not here, where the fuck would she go?"

"I have no idea. I don't really know her. To be honest, I don't know anyone who does."

"What about Saffron?"

"One step ahead of you. I also called her while I was waiting, and she said she couldn't think of anywhere."

I had no idea where to search. Isabel could be any-where—driving aimlessly along the coast, parked somewhere crying, heading back to Whitmore.

"Take me to Moonstone Beach," I said after we got in his truck. If there was anywhere someone would go and think, it made the most sense.

Snapper didn't question it. He just started the engine and drove.

Moonstone Beach sat at the edge of the world, where the land crumbled into tide pools and the Pacific stretched toward the horizon. The wind coming off the water was biting, carrying the smell of salt and kelp. I climbed out of the truck and made my way to one of the large boulders that overlooked the sand below.

While I didn't see my truck parked anywhere, maybe if I waited, Isabel would eventually come here too. It was the kind of place she'd be drawn to—beautiful and isolated, a place where she could disappear into herself without anyone watching. A place where the vastness of the ocean made human problems feel small.

I sat down on the damp stone and rested my fore-arms on my knees as I stared at the water. The waves rolled in, white-capped and relentless, crashing against the rocks below with a sound like distant thunder. Seabirds wheeled overhead, their cries sharp against the rush of the wind.

Isabel was out there somewhere. In my truck, driving God knew where, fleeing from the very thing she wanted most.

What Baron had said haunted my thoughts. *She's incapable of raising a child.*

He was wrong. I knew he was wrong with every fiber of my being. But sitting here, alone, with no idea where the woman I loved had gone, doubt threatened to creep in.

What if all my promises to stay, all my assurances that I'd be there no matter what, couldn't compete with a lifetime of damage? What if Isabel was too afraid to believe that anyone could love her the way she deserved to be loved?

The spray from the waves misted my face. I closed my eyes and breathed in the salt air, trying to steady myself.

I thought about finding her at Whitmore, sunburned and exhausted, with dirt under her fingernails and fire in her eyes. I thought about when she'd told me about the baby, when I'd held her hand and promised I wasn't going anywhere. I thought about last night—the fireplace, her whispered confession, how she trembled.

She *did* love me. I knew that. Whatever fear had driven her away today, it wasn't because she didn't. It was because she did—and that terrified her more than anything.

I got out my phone, tried her number again, and got the same result.

"Isabel." My voice cracked on her name. "I don't know where you are, but I need you to know something. I'm not giving up. I don't care how many times you run. I don't care how scared you get. I'm going to keep showing up until you believe me when I say I love you."

I paused, watching the waves crash against the rocks below. The sun was sinking lower now, casting long shadows across the sand. A pelican dove into the water and came up empty.

"I let you walk away once, and it was the biggest mistake of my life. I'm not doing it again. So wherever you are, please just…come back to me. Or tell me where you are, and I'll come to you. Just don't disappear. Not now. Not when we're so close to having everything."

I hung up and sat there as the light faded over the water.

Isabel was out there. I didn't know where, but I would find her. But I wouldn't quit searching. I loved her more than I'd ever known was possible.

I pushed myself off the boulder and walked back toward Snapper's truck. He stood near the hood, arms crossed, waiting with the patience that had always defined him.

"Ready?" he asked.

I looked back at the ocean, at the endless expanse of water and sky. "Yeah, let's go."

We climbed into the truck. As Snapper started the engine, my phone buzzed in my pocket. I yanked it out, heart pounding.

"Yeah?" I said, answering the call from a number I didn't recognize.

"Is this Rascon Avila?"

"It is."

"I'm calling about Isabel Van Orr."

14

Isabel

I drove without knowing where I was going.

Kick's truck seat was adjusted for his longer legs, and the mirrors were angled wrong. I gripped the steering wheel with both hands and turned onto the first road that led away from Los Caballeros, away from the Stonehouse, away from all those warm, welcoming faces that made me feel like I was drowning.

The vineyards blurred past my windows. Dormant vines stretched across the hills in neat rows, their bare branches reaching toward a sky I refused to look at. I knew this landscape. I'd grown up surrounded by it, had spent my whole life moving through wine country like a ghost—present but not quite real, visible but never seen.

My phone sat on the passenger seat where I'd tossed it. The screen was dark. I'd turned it off right before I fled.

Fled. I'd done it again. The one thing I'd promised myself I wouldn't do, and I'd done it anyway.

What Lucia said repeated again and again. *You're mine now. You're ours.*

My hands tightened on the wheel until my knuckles ached.

She meant to be kind. To welcome me. To give me the very thing I'd been starving for—unconditional acceptance from a parent who didn't keep score, didn't dangle love like a prize to be earned.

And I'd run from it like it was a threat.

Because that's what I did. That's who I was. The woman who couldn't accept kindness without waiting for the catch, who couldn't believe in belonging without bracing for the moment it would be snatched away.

I turned onto Vineyard Drive without thinking, then onto Adelaida Road, winding deeper into the hills. The afternoon sun cast long shadows across the pavement as I passed winery after winery—names I recognized, families I knew, an entire community that had watched me make a fool of myself year after year at the bachelor auction—worse, being a bitch to everyone who'd been kind to me.

My throat burned with tears I couldn't stop from falling, no matter how hard I tried.

"I'm sorry," I whispered.

My apology hung in the cab of the truck, absorbed by the leather seats and the faint smell of Kick that lingered everywhere. His jacket was draped over the back of the passenger seat. His sunglasses sat in the cupholder. His presence surrounded me even in his absence.

"I'm so sorry, baby girl."

My hand moved to my stomach without a conscious thought. At nineteen weeks, the swell was unmistakable now. I couldn't hide it anymore, not that I'd been trying. Not with Kick. Not with Thomas and Bas. Not with anyone who mattered.

The baby shifted inside me—a flutter, a ripple, like tiny bubbles rising through water. She'd been doing that more often lately, making her presence known in quiet moments when I least expected it.

"Your mama is a mess," I began. "You probably already figured that out. You've had a front-row seat to all of it—the crying, the worrying, the running away from people who were trying to love me."

Another flutter. I pressed my palm flat against the curve of my belly.

"I wanted to be different for you. I wanted to be better. When I found out about you, I promised myself I'd become someone worthy of being your mother. Someone who didn't make the same mistakes over and over. Someone who could accept love without destroying it."

The road curved through a section of oak trees, their branches bare and gnarled against the winter light. I slowed the truck to navigate the turn.

"And then your grandmother—your other grandmother, Kick's mom—she said things that spooked me. That I *belonged*. And I couldn't…I didn't know how to…"

I drew a shaky breath.

"I blamed your daddy. In my head, I was already doing it. Telling myself this was his fault for bringing me there, for putting me in that room with all those women, for making me face something I wasn't ready for."

The words came easier now, spilling out in the privacy of the truck cab, where no one could hear them except the baby I prayed would find it in her heart to forgive my shortcomings. My insecurities.

"It's what I do. I blame other people. My father taught me that—or maybe I just learned it from watching him. When something goes wrong, find someone else to hold responsible. When you can't handle your own feelings, make them someone else's fault."

I turned onto another road, this one narrower, less traveled. The vineyards gave way to pastureland, then back to vines again.

"But it's *not* his fault. None of this is his fault. Kick didn't make me run. He didn't make me panic. He didn't create the broken parts of me that can't accept love without waiting for it to be taken away."

I sounded steadier. The truth had a weight to it, a solidity that felt different from the lies I'd been telling myself.

"This is my pattern. My fear. I've been doing this my whole life—pushing people away before they can leave, running before anyone can reject me, convincing myself I don't deserve the things I want most."

The baby moved again, more insistent this time. I smiled despite the tears tracking down my cheeks.

"I know. I hear it too. How stupid it sounds when I say it out loud."

I reached an intersection, stopped, and let the engine idle while I tried to decide which way to go. Left led toward the coast. Right led deeper into wine country. Straight ahead led to town.

To Paso Robles. To the bar where everything had started between Kick and me.

"Two years ago," I said, "I met your daddy at a bar after the Wicked Winemakers' Ball. I was still wearing my fancy dress—no, wait, I'd changed. I'd gone back to my car and changed into jeans because I couldn't stand wearing that red gown for another minute. Couldn't stand being the woman I turned into when I wore clothes that felt more like armor."

I kept going straight, now that I had a destination in mind.

"I'd been there for a few minutes when he walked in. I can still see myself sitting at the bar, drinking bourbon on the rocks, knowing I looked like I wanted to be anywhere else but had nowhere to go." I took another deep breath. It was less shaky than the last. "We didn't like each other then. Or we thought we didn't. We'd spent years circling each other at events, making assumptions, and building walls."

The memory rose up, clear and sharp. The dim lighting. The smell of hops and old wood. Kick taking a seat at one end of the bar, while I was at the other, both of us pretending the other didn't exist until pretending became impossible.

"He got up first, walked over and sat on the stool beside me. Neither of us spoke for several minutes. And then, I told him things I'd never told anyone. About why I kept bidding on Snapper at the auction—how it was never about him, it was about winning, about feeling visible for one night a year. I let him see the real me in those few short hours we sat and drank together. The lonely, desperate, invisible me that I'd been hiding behind designer clothes and perfect hair."

I slowed as the outskirts of town appeared. Strip malls and gas stations, then older buildings with more character, then the downtown area with its tasting rooms, shops, and restaurants.

"He said I wasn't invisible. He looked right at me, and he said it like he meant it. Like he could actually see me."

The bar appeared on my right. Same weathered sign. Same small parking lot. Same unremarkable exterior that hid the place where my life had started to change.

I parked and, for several seconds, sat in the truck, staring at the entrance. The afternoon sun that filtered through the windshield felt warm on my face. My hand stayed pressed to my stomach, and the baby stayed quiet, as if she was waiting to see what I would do.

I could leave. I could turn the truck around and drive back to the Russian River Valley, back to Whitmore, back to the cottage where I'd built a new life. I could pretend this weekend had never happened, that I'd never gotten to know Kick's family, that I'd never felt the terrible weight of being offered everything I'd ever wanted.

Or I could walk into that bar and sit down and think. About me. About Kick. About our baby.

About my fucking father. About twenty-seven years of trying to earn his love, of twisting myself into shapes that might finally be good enough, of waiting for approval that never came. I'd spent my whole life waiting for Baron to choose me, and he never had. Not once.

But Kick had. Again and again. He'd tracked me down at Whitmore, refused to leave, claimed the baby as his before he even knew for certain. He'd held my hand in the hospital, talked to my stomach like our daughter could hear him, and looked at me like I was worth sticking around for.

He hadn't asked me to be anyone other than who I was. He hadn't required me to earn his acceptance or his presence. He'd just *stayed*.

And I'd kept running anyway.

"I'm done," I said. "I'm done blaming him. I'm done running. I'm done waiting for someone to prove they're going to leave so I can say I knew it all along."

I grabbed my purse from the passenger seat and climbed out of the truck.

The bar was mostly empty in the midafternoon lull. A couple sat at the far end, nursing beers and talking quietly. A man in a cowboy hat occupied a stool near the taps, watching a muted sports broadcast on the TV mounted in the corner. The bartender—a man I didn't recognize—wiped down glasses behind the counter.

I chose a booth near the back. The same booth where Kick and I had eventually ended up that night two years ago, after we'd stopped pretending we didn't want to talk to each other.

I slid onto the cracked leather bench and rested my hands on the table, palms down, like I was trying to ground myself.

The man from behind the bar appeared. "What can I get you?"

"Ginger ale, please."

"Wanna start a tab?"

I took my credit card from my purse. Not one my father controlled. One I'd gotten on my own that he didn't know about.

The guy took it and left without a comment. No judgment about a pregnant woman alone in a bar in the middle of the afternoon. No questions about why I looked like I'd been crying.

I stared at my phone's dark screen.

I could call him. I could dial his number and tell him where I was, make it easy, remove any uncertainty about whether he'd find me.

But that felt wrong. Too controlled. Too much like the old Isabel, the one who managed every situation, who never let anything happen without her explicit direction.

If Kick came, I wanted it to be because he'd looked for me. Because he knew me well enough to guess where I'd go. Because he refused to give up even when I gave him every reason to.

And if he didn't come…

I set the phone face-down on the table.

If he didn't come, I would still be here. I would still have stopped running. I would still have chosen to wait instead of flee, to stay instead of hide, to sit in the discomfort of uncertainty instead of sprinting toward the nearest exit.

That was the point. Not whether he showed up, but whether I could stay.

The man returned with my ginger ale. I wrapped my hands around the cold glass and watched the bubbles rise.

"This is where it started," I murmured, low enough that no one else could hear. "Me and your daddy. I felt like a different person that night. Like maybe I could be someone other than Baron Van Orr's disappointing daughter."

The baby stirred. A kick this time, sharp and definite.

"I know. I'm talking too much. But you're the only one who has to listen to me right now, and I need to say this out loud, or I'll lose my nerve."

I took a sip of the ginger ale. The fizz burned pleasantly against my throat.

"I love your daddy. I told him so last night, and I meant it. I whispered it because I was scared, but I said it. And he said it back—he said it first, actually, which was the braver thing. He's always been braver than me."

The afternoon light shifted as clouds moved across the sun. The bar grew dimmer for a moment, then brightened again.

"Your grandmother called me *mija*. Do you know what that means? My daughter. She looked at me, and she called me her daughter, and I couldn't breathe. Because my own mother never—"

I stopped. The tears were threatening again, and I was tired of crying.

"It doesn't matter. What matters is that I ran instead of staying. I ran instead of letting myself be loved."

I looked up at the clock behind the bar. An hour had passed since I'd fled the Stonehouse. Kick was probably frantic by now. Searching. Calling everyone he knew. Tearing apart the county, trying to find me.

Or maybe he wasn't. Maybe he'd finally had enough. Maybe watching me bolt from his family had shown him what everyone else already knew—that I was too broken, too damaged, too scarred to be worth the effort.

If that was true, I would survive it. I would be devastated, but I would survive. I had the baby. I had my work at Whitmore. I had a life I'd built on my own, independent of my father's money and approval.

I shook my head and rested one hand on my stomach. "Your daddy isn't the kind of man who gives up, and I shouldn't be, either."

I raised my glass, finished the ginger ale, then walked over to the bar to get my card.

What I was doing—waiting for him—was bullshit. He shouldn't have to find me. I should find him. Tell him how sorry I was. Pray he gave me another chance. Us another chance.

"I'll take the check now, please."

"It's on the house, Ms. Van Orr."

Behind me, I heard the door open and felt the warmth of the light that had spilled in. Or maybe it wasn't the sun's rays at all. Maybe it was the man I felt walking up to me. His warmth.

15

Kick

Snapper drove into the parking lot, and I had the door open before the truck stopped moving.

"Go get her," he said.

I didn't look back. I crossed the gravel lot in four strides and pushed through the door of the bar, my heart pounding so hard I could feel it in my throat.

She was standing with her back to me, one hand resting on the worn wood. Her hair was loose around her shoulders. She wore the same clothes she'd had on at the Stonehouse, but seeing her now, all I could think was how much I wanted to strip them off her, lay her down on our bed, join our bodies together, and pound my love into her so hard it would fill her up and she'd never forget it.

The door swung shut behind me, and the bartender's eyes flicked up, then back to the card in his hand. Isabel didn't turn around.

But I saw her shoulders shift. Saw the slight tilt of her head, the way her hand stilled on the counter.

She knew I was there.

I crossed the room in silence, weaving past the empty tables and scattered patrons who didn't look up from their drinks. When I reached her, I didn't say anything. I just slid my arms around her waist from behind and she rested against my chest.

She fit there like she'd been made for it. Like all those months of circling each other, of pretending we didn't feel this, had just been the long way home.

I pressed my mouth to her ear. "Goddamn, I love you, Isabel Van Orr."

A sound escaped her—half laugh, half sob. She still didn't turn around. She just relaxed into me, letting me take her weight, letting me hold her up.

"Take me home, Kick."

I tightened my arms around her, pressed a kiss to her temple, and breathed her in.

"Yeah," I said. "Let's go home."

The bartender slid her card across the counter. I reached past her to grab it, tucking it into her purse without letting go of her waist. She turned in my arms then, finally facing me, and I saw the tear tracks on her cheeks and the redness around her eyes.

"I was coming to find you," she said. "I was going to—"

I kissed her. Right there, in the middle of the bar, with the afternoon light slanting through the windows and the other patrons pretending not to watch. I kissed her because I'd spent the time since I found out she'd run from the Stonehouse thinking I might not get to do it again, and because, now, she was here and in my arms.

When I stepped away, her hands fisted in my jacket.

"Home," she said again.

I took her hand and led her outside.

We drove back to my house in silence, but it wasn't the cold silence of the ride to the airport from two months ago. This was so different. Her hand rested on my thigh the whole way, her fingers curled against my jeans like she needed the contact to believe I was real.

I kept one hand on the wheel and covered hers with the other.

The house was dark when we arrived. I parked in the garage, cut the engine, and we sat there for a moment in the quiet.

"How did you know where I was?"

"The bartender called. He knows everyone in wine country. Recognized you, probably from your card. He called a buddy who called a buddy, and eventually, it got to someone who had my number."

She laughed, quiet and tired. "Small towns."

"Small towns." I lifted her hand and pressed a kiss to her knuckles. "Come inside. We're gonna talk, Isabel, but not right away. First, we're gonna make love, and it may damn well take me all night to show you how much you fucking mean to me."

She didn't argue or deflect or do any of the things the old Isabel would have done. She just nodded, a look of hunger on her face that matched my own.

I led her inside, through the dark kitchen, and down the hallway to the bedroom. The house was cold, but I didn't care, and neither did she. We'd make our own warmth.

I stopped at the foot of the bed and turned to face her. In the dim light filtering through the window, she looked fragile. Breakable. But I knew better. This woman had survived things that would have crushed someone weaker. She just didn't know her own strength yet.

"I need you to hear something," I said. It came out rougher than I intended. "Before we do this. Before anything else."

She tilted her head, waiting.

"When I couldn't find you—when I didn't know where you were or if you were okay—I couldn't breathe. I tore through this county like a madman. I went to your father's house, Isabel. I confronted him. Because the thought of losing you…" I shook my head. "There is no version of my life that works without you in it. You understand? None."

Her breath caught. "Rascon—"

"I'm not done." I stepped closer and cupped her face in my hands. "You can run a thousand times. You can push me away, shut me out, build walls so high I can't see over them. And I will still be here. I will still come find you. I will still love you. That's not a promise I'm making. That's just the truth of who I am now."

A tear slipped down her cheek, and I caught it with my thumb.

"Now," I said, lowering my mouth toward hers. "Let me show you."

The kiss started soft. Tender. A question and an answer all at once. But it didn't stay that way. Her hands fisted in my shirt, and her gentleness gave way to raw hunger. Something that had been building since the moment I'd walked into that bar and seen her standing there.

I lifted her and rested her body on the mattress. She sat, then scooted back, making room for me. I followed her down, covering her body with mine, bracing my weight on my forearms so I wouldn't crush our daughter between us.

Our daughter. The thought hit me like it did every time—this impossible, miraculous reality that we'd made a life together. That she was carrying a piece of both of us inside her.

I kissed her deeper, my tongue sliding against hers, and she moaned into my mouth. Her hands found the hem of my shirt and tugged. I broke the kiss long enough to yank it over my head, then helped her with her sweater and her bra until she was bare from the waist up and the most beautiful thing I'd ever seen.

"I love you," I said against her stomach. "Both of you."

Isabel's fingers threaded through my hair. "Rascon. Please."

I knew what she needed. The same thing as me—to feel connected, to be as close as two people could get, to replace the fear of the last few hours with something solid and real.

I unzipped her jeans and worked them down her hips, taking her underwear with them. She lay beneath me, naked and trembling, her chest rising and falling with quickened breaths. I stripped the rest of my clothes off and settled between her thighs.

"Look at me," I said.

Her eyes met mine. Dark. Wanting. Trusting.

I put my hands between her legs and felt her wet heat, then slid into her slowly, watching her face and the way her lips parted and her lashes fluttered. She was so warm, so tight, so fucking perfect that I had to stop and breathe, or it would be over before it started.

"You feel that?" I pressed in again, deeper. "This is where I belong. Right here. With you."

She wrapped her legs around my waist, drawing me closer. "Then, stay."

"Always."

I set a rhythm—slow at first, savoring every stroke, every sound she made. Her nails raked down my back, and her hips rose to meet mine. We moved together like we'd been doing this for years instead of months, like our bodies had memorized each other.

I buried my face in her neck, breathing her in and kissing the hollow of her throat, the curve of her shoulder, and the spot behind her ear that made her gasp.

"I've got you," I murmured against her skin. "I've got you, baby. Let go."

She shattered beneath me, her whole body arching off the mattress, my name on her lips. I followed her over the edge, spilling into her with a groan that came from somewhere deep in my chest.

I stayed inside her, our bodies still joined, our hearts pounding in tandem, her fingers tracing lazy patterns on my back.

"I love you," she whispered. There was no hesitation this time, particularly when she repeated it. "I love you, Rascon."

I kissed her forehead. Her nose. Her lips. "I know. I love you too."

We lay together afterward, her head on my chest, my hand stroking up and down her spine. The room had warmed from our bodies, from the heat we'd generated, but I covered us with the blanket anyway.

"Tell me what happened," I said. "At the lunch."

She was quiet, then took a deep breath, and told me—about the things my mother said to her, about feeling like she was drowning in kindness she didn't know how to accept. She didn't belabor it. Didn't explain every thought that had run through her head. She just gave me the shape of it, and I filled in the rest.

"Your mother offered me something I've wanted my whole life," she said. "And I didn't know how to take it. So I ran."

"And then you stopped."

"And then I stopped." She lifted her head to look at me. "I went to that bar because it's where we started. I figured…if you were going to find me, you'd look there."

"I would have looked everywhere." I tucked a strand of hair behind her ear. "But I'm glad you made it easy."

A ghost of a smile crossed her face. "Where did you look? Before the bartender called?"

"As I said, I went to your father's place. I thought maybe that was where you'd gone. You hadn't, thank God, but he was there, and we had words."

"What do you mean?"

"I made it clear he doesn't get to have opinions about us. About our family. About how we raise our daughter."

She studied my face. I wondered what she was looking for—anger, maybe, or regret. She wouldn't find either.

"Our daughter?"

"He knows about the pregnancy, Isabel. Are you surprised?"

She shook her head. "What did he say?"

"Nothing worth repeating." I kissed her temple. "He doesn't matter. You matter. Our baby matters. This—" I gestured at the space between us, at the tangled sheets and the warmth we'd made. "This is what matters."

She rested her head on my chest. "I want to go back to Whitmore."

"Me too."

"When?"

"Right now, if that's what you want. You can sleep on the way."

She looked up at me. "You wouldn't mind?"

"I'd rather be there than here. The farther you are from Baron, the better I'll feel."

"Can we stop at your mom's on the way?"

I blinked. "Are you sure?"

"I am. I need to apologize for the way I left." She took a breath. "I don't want them to think I don't want to be part of your family. I do. I just panicked. And they deserve to hear that from me."

Pride swelled in my chest. I knew how hard this was for her—how every instinct she had was screaming at her to avoid her vulnerabilities.

But she was doing it anyway.

"Yeah," I said. "We can stop."

The house was lit up when we arrived, warm light spilling from every window. Multiple cars in the drive-way meant the women hadn't dispersed after the lunch.

Isabel's hand found mine as we walked up the path. Her grip was tight enough to hurt.

"You've got this," I said.

"I might throw up."

"I'll hold your hair."

She shot me a look that was half glare, half grati-tude. Then she squared her shoulders and knocked.

Ma answered. Her eyes went wide when she saw Isabel, then soft with relief.

"Oh, *mija*," she said. "Come in. Both of you."

Isabel flinched but didn't bolt. She let my mother lead her inside, into the warmth and light of the living room where the other women waited.

They were all there—Saffron on one end of the sofa, Alex with a wineglass, Jaicon and Addison sharing the loveseat, Eberly perched on the arm of a chair, and Ainsley cross-legged on the floor near Daphne. They looked up when Isabel entered.

"I owe you all an apology," she began. "I shouldn't have left the way I did. You were all so kind to me, and I repaid that kindness by disappearing. That was wrong, and I'm sorry."

Silence filled the room.

Then Alex spoke up. "Honey, sit down. You look like you're about to face a firing squad, and the only thing we're armed with is wine and leftover dessert."

A few women laughed. Isabel blinked.

"We're a lot," my sister continued. "I know that. I'm a lot all by myself—just ask Kick, he'll give you an itemized list of all the things I do to make him and the rest of our brothers crazy. Add in all these other personalities, and it's overwhelming."

"I still get nervous," Eberly admitted. "Last Christmas, I locked myself in the bathroom for twenty minutes and pretended I had a stomach bug."

Addison nodded. "There are days when I need to hide in the pantry just to catch my breath."

"The bathroom by the kitchen has the best acoustics for crying," Daphne offered. "Very soothing echo."

Isabel's rigid posture softened. "I thought you'd be angry."

Ma moved forward and took Isabel's hands. "We could never be angry with you for feeling too much. I told you that you're part of our family now—and that means we give you grace when you need it. All we ask is that you eventually come back."

Isabel's composure cracked. I watched the tears spill over, and I had to fight the urge to go to her. This wasn't my moment. This was hers.

"I don't know how to do this," she whispered. "I never learned."

"Then, we'll teach you," Ma said. "That's what family is for."

She pulled Isabel into a hug, and after a moment, Isabel hugged her back and her shoulders shook. The other women gathered around—not crowding, but present. Saffron put a hand on her back. Ainsley squeezed her arm. Even Alex reached out to touch her shoulder.

I stood in the doorway and watched the woman I loved let herself be held by the family she'd been too afraid to claim.

We didn't get back to Whitmore until almost midnight.

Isabel fell asleep somewhere around King City, her head against the window, one hand on her belly. I reached over and covered it with mine.

We were going to be okay. All three of us.

When we reached the cottage, she woke as I cut the engine.

"We're home," she murmured.

"We're home."

We stumbled inside together, too tired for anything but sleep. She climbed into bed and reached for me, and I went to her.

She curled against my chest, her leg over mine, her arm around my waist, and the baby nestled between us.

"Thank you," she murmured. "For coming to find me."

"Always. That's the deal."

"What deal?"

"The one where I show up. Every time. No matter what."

She tilted her head up and kissed my jaw. "I'm going to hold you to that."

"Counting on it."

As her breathing slowed, I lay in the darkness, holding her, and let myself believe we'd finally gotten over a huge hurdle. Today had been a turning point. Not just for her, but for me too. I'd never doubt that Isabel wanted me or loved me. I knew she did, and each time she needed me to, that's the knowledge I'd act with.

And tomorrow, we'd figure out the rest. No matter what, though, I knew we'd be okay.

16

Kick

I woke to the sound of my phone buzzing on the nightstand.

For a moment, I didn't move. Isabel was still curled against me, her breath warm on my chest and her hand resting over my heart. Light filtered through the curtains, soft and gray. It was barely dawn. I didn't want to disturb this—the peace we'd finally found, the quiet after the storm.

But my phone buzzed again.

I reached for it carefully, trying not to wake her, and saw a text from Thomas.

Need to see you at the main house. Urgent.

I frowned. Thomas wasn't the type for dramatics. If he said urgent, he meant it.

I eased out from under Isabel, replacing my body with a pillow so she wouldn't wake to cold sheets. She murmured something in her sleep and burrowed deeper into the blankets, one hand moving to rest on her belly. I stood there for a moment, watching her. The woman

I loved. The mother of my child. Safe and warm and finally, finally mine.

I put on jeans and a sweatshirt, shoved my feet into boots, and headed out.

The walk to the main house took less than five minutes. The vineyard stretched out on either side of the path, its dormant vines reaching toward a sky heavy with clouds. The air was cold and damp, carrying the promise of rain. I shoved my hands in my pockets and picked up my pace.

The main house was a sprawling Victorian that had been in the Whitmore family for generations. Thomas had restored it himself over the years, and it showed— every detail was perfect, from the wraparound porch to the stained glass windows flanking the front door.

I knocked and waited.

Footsteps sounded inside, then the door swung open to reveal Bas, half asleep, hair sticking up on one side, wearing sweatpants and a wrinkled T-shirt. He blinked at me, then rubbed his eyes.

"Kick." He stifled a yawn and ushered me inside. "I saw you guys come back late last night. Izzy's okay?"

The casual use of her nickname—the one only certain people were allowed to use—didn't bother me the way it might have a month ago. "She's good. We're good. And shit, I'm sorry I didn't get back to you yesterday. There was just…a lot."

"Glad you found her." He rested against the wall. "So, if that's all you came by to tell me, then next time, wait until a decent fucking hour, would you?" He squinted past me at the sky. "I mean, what time is it?"

"Uh, a little after six?"

"Jesus." He pushed me out of the way so he could open the door. "Go back to bed, Avila. It's way too early for this shit."

I laughed, but it faded quickly. "Yeah, well, I'm not here to apologize. Even though I should be." I took out my phone and showed him the text. "I'm here because your father asked me to come up to the house."

Bas frowned at the screen. "My father?"

"That's right."

"Kick, my dad's not here." Bas straightened, suddenly more awake. "He meets a bunch of his buddies for breakfast in town every week. They get together at dawn, of all the ridiculous times. He left over an hour ago."

We stared at each other.

The realization hit us both at the same moment.

"Oh my God," Bas breathed.

I was already turning, already running, my boots pounding against the porch steps, the gravel path, the wet grass between the main house and the cottage. Behind me, I heard Bas swear, heard the door slam behind him, but I didn't wait. I couldn't wait.

The cottage door was open. Not ajar. Not cracked. Wide open, swinging gently in the morning breeze.

"Isabel!" I tore through the house. "Isabel!"

The bedroom was empty. The sheets were tangled and still warm when I pressed my hand to them. Her clothes from yesterday were draped over the chair. Her purse sat on the dresser, her phone beside it.

Bas appeared in the doorway, breathless, his feet shoved into unlaced boots. "She's not—"

"No!" The word came out raw. Broken. "She's not here."

"The security cameras." Bas was already reaching for his phone. "Dad has cameras all over the property."

His face went pale.

"What?" I grabbed the device out of his hand. "Let me see."

I watched the footage with my heart in my throat. The time stamp showed five minutes ago, and I watched as Isabel walked out of the cottage.

Isabel, walking out of the cottage. She was wearing my T-shirt—the one she'd slept in—and a pair of jeans she must have put on in a hurry. Rubber boots, the kind we wore in the vineyards, were on her feet. A man walked beside her, tall and broad-shouldered, dressed in black. His hand rested on her elbow. Not gripping. Guiding.

She wasn't struggling. Wasn't fighting. She walked to a dark SUV parked as close as it could get to the porch and climbed in without looking back.

I watched it three times. Four. Looking for something—a signal, a sign, anything that would tell me what had happened in those moments before the camera caught her.

The fifth time, I saw it.

Just before she climbed into the SUV, her hand moved to her stomach. A quick, protective gesture. She pressed her palm flat against the swell of our daughter, and then she got in the vehicle and was gone.

To anyone else, it would look like she left willingly.

But I knew better. There was no way she'd leave me. Not by choice. Not after everything that happened yesterday. She was protecting the baby. She was doing whatever they asked because someone had threatened our child.

"She didn't run," I said. Of that, I was certain.

"I know."

"She wouldn't leave without her phone. Without her purse."

"I know, Kick."

I rewound the footage. Watched it again. The way Isabel held herself, spine straight, chin up. The way she didn't look back at the cottage.

She was scared. She was complying. And there was only one reason she would do that.

"They threatened something," I said. "They threatened me. Or the baby. That's the only way she'd go with them."

Bas nodded. "That's what I thought too."

"Baron." The name tasted like poison. "He had us followed. From Paso Robles. He knew exactly where we were."

I handed the phone back to Bas and paced. I didn't know where to start. What to do. There was only one thing I was certain of beyond knowing Isabel was forced to leave—I needed Los Caballeros, and I needed them now.

I called Snapper. He answered on the first ring, and three minutes later, he said he'd call the minute they got to the airfield and were on their way. I didn't know who he meant by "they," and I didn't care.

"My father's on his way back. The sheriff is with him, and he's making calls."

The sheriff? Making calls? I couldn't think straight. Blood rushed through my veins, and I felt like I was going to crawl out of my skin.

"He's trying to determine what resources Baron has, who he might have hired." Bas looked up at me. "We should go back to the house."

"Give me a minute." I searched every room of the cottage, looking for anything at all that Isabel might've left as a clue, but nothing looked new or out of place.

Just as we walked into the house, Thomas arrived with a man he introduced as Clayton Boone.

"I've got deputies on their way," he said as he shook my hand.

"You're the sheriff?" I asked since he was dressed in plain clothes.

He may have responded, but I didn't hear him when my cell buzzed with a call from my brother.

"Snapper? Talk to me."

"We just boarded at Paso Robles Municipal. Flight time on the Cessna is under thirty minutes. Press arranged for a helicopter to get us at the Sonoma Country Airfield, so we'll be to you in under an hour at the most. In the meantime, we're calling in every favor from everyone we know."

I thanked him and ended the call.

Thomas, Bas, and Clayton were all head-to-head and on their phones. An alert sounded, and Bas raced into another room. I followed him. On the monitor, I saw Press at the gate. "That's Lavery Barrett," I told him. Bas pressed a button on his cell, and the gate opened. Press arrived seconds later, and I met him outside.

"We'll find her," he said, pulling me into a quick embrace.

"Baron is behind this. I fucking know he is," I seethed.

"There is no question," he responded as I led him inside.

"I think I know where he took her," Bas said, spinning in my direction when we walked inside.

"Where?"

He ran a hand through his hair. For a moment, he looked younger than his years. Lost. "Miremont."

"Why would she go there? I thought her father sold it."

Bas' brow furrowed. "That's what she told me too."

Press was typing something on his phone. "That's what I'd heard too," he muttered. "But Baron did *not* sell it. It's still one of the Van Orr Corp's holdings."

"That motherfucking *sonuvabitch*," Bas said under his breath. "He lied to her about it?" He turned to his father, who nodded.

"I've heard rumors that Baron kept the property. Let it go dormant. Closed the winery and fired the staff," said Thomas. "But I never confirmed it because it wasn't my business…" His eyes met mine. "I'd be willing to bet this entire place—the winery, the vineyards, all of it—that's where he took her."

"Where is it?"

"Let's go!" I shouted, racing toward the door.

"Hold on, son," said the sheriff, blocking my way. "Let's think about how we're going to approach this."

"The fuck I will." I tried to get around him, but Press grabbed my arm.

Thomas shook his head. "You have to understand something about Baron Van Orr. I've known him for forty years. We were best friends before things went wrong between us. And in all that time, I've never seen him admit he was wrong about anything. Not once."

"I don't give a damn about his psychology," I snapped.

"You should. Because it's the key to predicting what else he'll do." Thomas rested his hands on the desk in front of him. "Baron has always believed he knows what's best for Isabel. He's spent her whole life controlling her—her money, her choices—Baron had a hand in all of it. And when she stepped out of line, he punished her. Not with violence. With withdrawal. With silence and money. With the constant reminder that his love was conditional on her obedience."

I thought about Isabel's face when she'd talked about her father. The way she flinched at kindness because she'd learned to expect there'd be strings attached. The way she ran from love because she'd been taught that staying meant getting hurt.

Baron hadn't just controlled her. He'd broken something in her. Something she was only now learning to rebuild.

"When she stopped playing by his rules," Thomas continued, "when she chose you, when she got pregnant with a baby he can't control, by a man he can't buy, he snapped. In his mind, he's probably convinced himself he's protecting her. Saving her from a mistake. He doesn't see what he's doing as wrong. He sees it as necessary."

"Necessary?" I snarled. "By kidnapping her? By ripping her away from the people who actually love her?"

"I'm not defending him, Kick. I'm explaining him. And I'm telling you that a man like Baron—a man who can justify anything to himself—is dangerous. He won't respond to threats. He won't back down because you're angry. The only thing that will reach him is being held accountable by people he can't dismiss." Thomas' eyes bored into mine. "You know *who* and *what* I'm talking about."

"I do," I said. "And they're on their way."

I thought about my confrontation with Baron yesterday. The things he'd said about Isabel giving up the baby. The cold certainty in his eyes when he'd told me I wasn't good enough for her.

He'd been planning this. Even then. He'd looked me in the face, knowing his people were already in position to take her.

"I'm going to kill him," I said.

"No, you're not." Press stepped in front of me, his hand on my chest. "You're going to keep your head. You're going to let us handle this the right way. And you're going to bring Isabel home safe." He looked at his phone. "They've landed."

My eyes opened wide. "Bas, you said Miremont is south of here, right?"

"Yes."

"Closer to the airport."

Bas nodded.

"Tell them to meet us there instead of coming here," I said to Press.

He got on his phone, and I looked from Bas to his father, then to his sheriff. "I can't wait around. If we think there's a chance that's where Isabel is, I need to go. Now."

Thomas looked at Clayton, who nodded. "I've got units on the way. Silent pursuit for now."

My eyes met Press', and we raced out to his SUV.

"I'm coming with you," Bas shouted, climbing in the rear passenger seat.

Thomas came out and stood directly in front of the SUV. "Wait," he said, resting both hands on the hood. "You need to coordinate with the others. If you go charging in without a plan, you could make things worse. Baron has resources. Security. If he feels cornered, there's no telling what he might do."

"I don't care about—"

"Isabel would care," said Thomas. "She would want you to be smart about this. She would want you to protect her and your baby. Don't let your anger make you reckless."

I closed my eyes and drew a breath. He was right. I hated that he was right, but he was.

"Tryst is coordinating," Press said. "We rendezvous with them at Gracianna Vineyards."

"That's perfect," said Bas. "There's a mountain between them. If they're there, Baron won't see anyone coming."

"And what if Baron's already gone by the time we get there?" I asked.

"Then, we figure out where he went next. But *think* about it, Kick," Bas urged.

"You're right. He'll try to convince her she's better off without me. Break her down until she agrees to come back under his control." My hands clenched into fists. "That's not going to happen."

"No," Press agreed. "It's not."

Thomas moved away from the SUV. "Let's roll, boys."

The drive south felt endless.

I sat in the passenger seat, my phone pressed to my ear, coordinating with Tryst. Bas, behind me, stared silently out the window.

Every mile felt like ten. I studied the security footage he'd sent to my phone, watching Isabel walk away from me, watching her hand move to her stomach, watching her disappear into that SUV.

Why hadn't I fucking ignored Thomas' message? Why hadn't I questioned it? Why in the ever-living hell had I left her alone for even five minutes?

"Stop." Press speaking cut through my spiral. "I can hear you thinking from here, and it's not helping."

"I should have—"

"You couldn't have known. No one could have known. Baron planned this, and he planned it well. Beating yourself up won't get her back faster."

Whether Press was right or wrong, guilt sat in my chest like a stone, heavy and cold and impossible to ignore.

"When he told her he sold it, she cried for a week. Called me at three in the morning, drunk, saying she'd lost the last piece of her mother she had left." I turned to look at Bas over the seat as he spoke. "That's when I knew what kind of man Baron was."

I felt my hatred for Baron sharpen into something colder. More focused.

"She won't let him break her. Not now. Not when she finally has something worth fighting for," Bas added.

"She's always had things worth fighting for. She just didn't believe she deserved them." I looked over at Press. "Drive…fucking…faster."

He pushed the accelerator down, eating up the miles between us and the woman we were going to save.

I closed my eyes. *Hang on, Isabel. I'm coming. No matter what it takes, I'm coming for you and for our baby.*

17

Isabel

The man at my bedroom door was polite.

That was the thing I kept coming back to during the drive and after. He didn't yell, grab, or threaten me. He just stood in the doorway of the bedroom in the cottage I'd thought of as home last night, blocking the gray morning light, and said, "Ms. Van Orr. Your father sent us. We need you to come with us now."

I was still half asleep, still reaching for the warmth Kick had left behind. The pillow he'd tucked against me was a poor substitute for his body, and I'd been drifting back toward consciousness, vaguely aware that he'd left, vaguely planning to get up and find him.

And then there was a stranger in my bedroom.

I sat up, pulling the blankets to my chest. "Get out. I'm not going anywhere with you."

The man didn't move. Behind him, I could see another figure in the hallway. Two of them. Maybe more.

"Ms. Van Orr." He sounded almost kind. "Your father anticipated your reluctance. He asked me to tell you that if you don't come willingly, we'll wait for Mr. Avila to return. And we'll make sure he understands how serious your father is about bringing you home."

My blood went cold.

"What does that mean?"

"It means your father has resources, Ms. Van Orr. And he's prepared to use them. Mr. Avila seems like a good man. It would be a shame if something happened to him."

I had no idea where Kick was, only that he'd left. When he returned, he'd be unsuspecting and unarmed, walking into an ambush, because of me.

"You have five minutes to get dressed," the man said. "I suggest you use them."

I used two.

I put on a sweatshirt and jeans, shoved my feet into the rubber boots by the door, and walked out of the cottage without looking back. I didn't take my phone. I didn't take my purse. I didn't leave a note. There wasn't time, and even if there had been, I didn't want to give them any reason to stay. Any reason to be here when Kick came back.

The SUV was waiting right outside. I climbed in without being told. One of the men sat beside me in the back. Another drove while a third sat in the passenger seat in front of me.

We left Whitmore as the sun crept over the hills, and I watched the cottage disappear in the side mirror. Watched the vineyards blur past. Watched the life I'd been building shrink to nothing behind me.

I pressed my hand to my stomach. Our daughter shifted beneath my palm, restless, as if she could sense my fear.

"It's okay," I said silently. "We're going to be okay."

I didn't believe it. But I said it anyway, because that's what mothers were supposed to do. Give comfort. Not that mine ever had.

The drive was shorter than I expected.

We wound through back roads, past vineyards I didn't recognize, until we turned onto a private drive marked by a stone pillar half hidden by overgrown hedges. The name carved into the stone was weathered, barely legible.

Miremont.

My heart stopped when he drove through the gates of the place I'd always believed would become mine when my mother passed away.

Then, a few months after she did, my father told me he'd sold it. He said the upkeep was too expensive, the property too far from our other holdings, and the memories too painful. He'd taken the money and invested it "on my behalf." Every cent of which he controlled.

I'd grieved this place like a death. Like losing my mother all over again.

The SUV rolled up the long drive, past rows of dormant vines that had clearly been neglected for years. Weeds choked the spaces between the rows. The trellis wires sagged. The cover crops had gone wild, reclaiming the land in tangled masses of brown and green.

But the bones were still there. The gentle slope of the hillside. The old stone walls that marked the property boundaries. The winery building in the distance, its windows dark, its doors chained shut.

And the house.

The house where my mother had spent her summers as a girl. The house where she'd married my father in the garden, surrounded by roses and grapevines and all the hope of a young bride who didn't yet know what her husband would become.

The house looked as abandoned as everything else. Paint peeled from the shutters, and the gardens were overgrown. The fountain in the circular drive was dry and cracked.

But lights glowed in the windows. Someone was here. Someone was waiting.

The SUV stopped, and the man beside me opened my door.

"Your father is inside," he said. "He's looking forward to seeing you."

I climbed out on legs that didn't feel steady. I stood there for a moment, staring at the house that should have been mine, and felt something crack open in my chest.

Not grief. Not anymore.

Rage.

Baron was waiting in the room I remembered my mother referring to as the parlor.

He stood by the fireplace, one hand resting on the mantle, the other holding a glass of what looked like whiskey. He was dressed immaculately, as always—dark suit, silk tie, shoes polished to a mirror shine. He looked like a man receiving guests for brunch, not one who'd just had his pregnant daughter kidnapped.

"Isabel." He set the glass down and crossed to me, arms open as if expecting an embrace.

I stepped back before he could touch me. "You told me you sold it," I spat at him.

"I said what needed to be said at the time." He lowered his arms, his expression smoothing into something patient. Paternal. The face he wore when he was about to explain why he knew better than everyone else. "You were twenty-two. You'd just lost your mother. You were in no state to manage a property of this size."

"So you lied to me."

"I protected you."

"From what?" My tone hardened. I couldn't stop it. "From my own inheritance? From the one thing my mother left me—the one thing that was supposed to be *mine*?"

"From yourself." Baron's tone hardened. "You would have run this place into the ground within a year. You had no experience, no discipline, no understanding of what it takes to manage a working vineyard. Your mother's family made the mistake of leaving it to you without conditions. I corrected that mistake."

"You *stole* it from me."

"I held it in trust for you, Isabel. You can cease these dramatics."

"*In trust for me?* You watched me grieve this place—watched me cry after you told me it was gone—and you said nothing. You let me believe the last piece of my mother's family had been sold to strangers, and the whole time, it was sitting here. Empty. Abandoned. Because you'd rather let it rot than let me have something that was mine."

"The property required significant investment. You weren't capable—"

"I wasn't capable because you never *let* me be capable." As I spoke, it felt like a dam breaking after years of pressure. "Every time I tried to do something on my own, you undermined me. You kept me dependent on you, and then you used that dependence as proof that I couldn't survive without you."

Baron's expression flickered. Just for a second. "Everything I did was for your own good."

"No. Everything you did was so you could control me. You made me into the spoiled princess everyone sees—and then you punished me for being her. You created the very thing you claim to despise."

I gestured at the room around us. The dusty furniture. The faded wallpaper. The portraits of my mother's family hanging on walls that should have been mine to care for.

"How could you?"

"I did what I always do—saved you from the embarrassment of failing publicly, the way you've failed at everything else."

He might as well have slapped me. I'd heard this same rhetoric my entire life. You're not ready. You're not capable. You're not good enough. Hearing it all again now felt different. Sharper. More brutal.

Because I wasn't the same woman I'd been a year ago. Six months ago. Even six weeks ago.

"I've been working," I said. "At Whitmore. Actually working. In the vineyard. With the crew." I held up my hands, showing him the calluses on my palms. "For the first time in my life, I have proof that I can do something other than spend your money. And you know what? I'm good at it. Thomas says I have excellent instincts. The crew respects me. I've earned something real, something that has nothing to do with you."

Baron's gaze flicked to my hands, then back to my face. His expression didn't change. "Playing in the dirt doesn't make you a vintner, Isabel. It makes you a dilettante. A rich girl pretending to be something she's not."

"I'm not pretending anymore. That's what scares you, isn't it? That I might actually become someone who doesn't need you. Someone who can stand on her own."

"You got yourself pregnant." He sounded bitter, cold. "By a rodeo cowboy with no ambition and no future. You ran away from your family, your responsibilities, your life—and you think playing farmhand for a few weeks makes you independent?"

"There is no money." I stepped closer to him, close enough to see the way his jaw tightened. "You cut me off, remember? You told me another scandal and I was done. Well, here I am. Pregnant. Unmarried. Living with the father of my child. Every scandal you warned me about, all at once. And you know what happened?"

I waited. He didn't answer.

"He *stayed*." My voice cracked. "Kick stayed. Not because of money—there isn't any. Not because of status or connections or any of the things you think matter. He stayed because he loves me. Because he wants to be a father to our daughter. Because when I pushed him away, he refused to go."

"He's using you."

"For what?" My laugh sounded harsh and bitter. "I have nothing. You made sure of that. You said it yourself. I have no trust fund, no inheritance, no access to Van Orr money. I'm worthless by your standards. And he stayed anyway."

I thought about Kick tracking me to Whitmore when I'd lied about going to Italy. Refusing to leave even when I begged him to. Holding my hand in the hospital when I thought I was losing the baby, his demeanor steady even though I could see the fear in his eyes.

I thought about his mother calling me *mija*. About Alex and his sisters-in-law making room for me at their table. About a whole family opening their arms to a woman who'd given them no reason to even like her.

"He stayed," I said. "And he never once made me feel like I had to earn his love."

I wiped my eyes again.

"You wouldn't recognize love because you've never given it. Not to me anyway. Maybe you did to my mother. But you made sure she held herself away from me too. You took control and manipulated her."

I felt sick to my stomach and relieved at the same time when he didn't deny it.

I looked up at the person I no longer thought of as my father. He was just a man. As if it happened in an instant, he looked pale, almost frail, to me now. I'd never spoken to him the way I was. I'd never yelled, never pushed back, never said the things that had been building inside me since I was old enough to feel the pain of his wrath.

But I wasn't finished.

"My mother died, and you disappeared." Years of grief and anger rose to the surface. "I was twenty-two years old and an orphan. She wasn't the only one who died; you might as well have too."

Baron's hand shook, and he set his glass on a table beside him.

"I needed a father. I needed someone to tell me it was going to be okay, that we would get through it together. And you gave me a checkbook. You gave me a credit card and a pat on the head, and you sent me away because you couldn't stand to look at me."

"That's not true—"

"I look just like her." My voice broke. "I know that. Every time you looked at me, you saw her. And you couldn't stand it. You wished she were still alive. If

you could have, you would've traded my life for hers in a heartbeat."

"I was grieving—"

"So was I!" I shouted. "And you let me know in no uncertain terms that I would vanish into thin air. No longer be a weight of responsibility around your neck. No longer be a reminder of the one person you actually loved."

I wiped my eyes with the back of my hand. I hadn't meant to cry. Hadn't wanted to give him that. But the tears came anyway.

"I spent my whole life waiting for something you're incapable of giving. The sadder part is, neither of you was capable of it," I said. "But I'm done. I found someone who fills all the empty spaces inside of me, and to him, it comes naturally because he *loves* me."

"Isabel—"

"I'm keeping my baby." My hand moved to my stomach. "I'm staying with Kick. I'm building a life that has nothing to do with you. You're as dead to me as my mother is."

Baron's face was closed off as if he felt nothing. As if what I'd said meant nothing.

"You're overly emotional," he said. "You're not thinking clearly. It's the pregnancy—hormones, stress. Once you've had time to calm down, you'll see that I'm right."

"I've never been more clear on anything in my life."

"We're leaving." He moved toward the door, gesturing for me to follow. "The plane is waiting. We'll go to Italy, to the villa. You can rest there, away from all this chaos. Away from him. And when the baby comes, we'll discuss options."

"Options?" I didn't move. "What options?"

"Adoption. A good family. People who can give the child what it deserves." He spoke as if he were discussing a business arrangement rather than my baby's future. "You're not ready to be a mother, Isabel. You know that. Deep down, you know."

I stared at him and shook my head. The only thing I felt for this man was pity. "I used to think that," I said quietly. "I used to believe every terrible thing you said about me. That I was spoiled. Selfish. Incapable of doing anything worthwhile. But you know what? I was wrong. And so were you."

I walked toward him, and for the first time in my life, I saw him take a step back.

"I'm going to be a good mother. Not because of anything you taught me about parenting—but because I know exactly what *not* to do. I know how it feels to be invisible to your own father. I know how it feels to beg for scraps of affection and get nothing. My child will never feel that way. She will know, every single day of her life, that she is loved. Unconditionally. Without strings."

I reached the doorway and turned back to face him.

"You have a choice. This is the only time I'm going to make this offer. You can let me walk out of here. Tell your goons to take me back to Whitmore. You can apologize to me for all of it. If you do that, I'll let you be a part of my life. Our life."

Baron's jaw tightened. For a moment—just a moment—I thought I saw something crack behind his eyes. Something human. Something hurt.

Then it was gone.

"We'll discuss this on the plane, when you've had time to—"

"I'm not getting on a plane with you."

"Isabel." His voice hardened. "I'm not asking."

He stepped forward, gripped my arm, and steered me toward the front door. His fingers dug into my flesh—not enough to bruise, but enough to remind me that he was still stronger than me. Still in control.

I didn't fight him. There was no point. The men who'd brought me here were probably still outside, waiting to make sure I did what I was told.

But as Baron opened the front door and pushed me onto the porch, I realized something had changed.

I wasn't afraid anymore.

Not of him. Not of what he might do. Not of the future I couldn't predict.

I'd said everything I needed to say. I'd finally told the truth—to him and to myself. Whatever happened next, I would face it as the woman I'd become. Not the scared little girl who'd spent her life begging for her parents' love.

That girl was gone.

And then I looked up.

The circular drive that had been empty when I arrived was now full of people—men. They were standing in a loose semicircle around the house.

And in the center of them, his eyes locked on mine, was Kick.

He looked wrecked. Pale. Furious. His hands were clenched at his sides, and even from twenty feet away,

I could see the tension vibrating through his body—the barely restrained violence of a man who'd been ready to tear the world apart to find me.

Beside him stood Snapper. And Bas, of all people, his face tight with worry. There were more. All of Kick's brothers and friends. And the hardest part for my father was that his friends were here too. Men I knew he respected. Them witnessing what he was doing to me would bring him far more shame than I ever had.

His grip on my arm went slack.

His eyes scrunched. "What is this?"

Tryst stepped forward. His expression was calm, but his eyes were hard as flint.

"Baron," he said. "We need to have a conversation. About the code you swore to uphold and the woman you just tried to take from one of our own."

I jerked my arm free from my father's grip and ran toward Kick.

18

Kick

Isabel ran toward me, and the world narrowed to the space between us.

I caught her in my arms, pulling her against my chest so hard I worried about the baby. But I couldn't let go. She was shaking, her entire body trembling as she pressed her face into my shoulder, and I wrapped myself around her like I could absorb the fear right out of her.

"I've got you," I said against her hair. "I've got you."

Her fingers dug into my back. She didn't cry. She just stayed there, breathing in ragged bursts that slowly steadied.

Over her head, I watched Baron Van Orr standing on his own porch, staring at the men who had gathered in his driveway. His face had gone pale. Not with fear—Baron wasn't capable of that—but with the dawning realization that he'd miscalculated. That his money and influence couldn't buy his way out of what he'd done.

Tryst stepped forward, and the other *Viejos* moved with him. Men who had known Baron for decades. Men whose respect he had cultivated his entire adult life.

"Baron." Tryst's voice carried across the space between them, calm, measured, and devastating in its quiet authority. "We need to have a conversation…"

Baron's jaw tightened. "This is a family matter. My daughter—"

"Your daughter is standing in the arms of a man who loves her." Tryst spoke softly. He didn't need to shout. "A man who came here with his brothers and his friends to bring her home. You don't get to call this a family matter when you're the one who made it something else entirely."

I felt Isabel shift in my arms, turning her head to watch her father. I loosened my grip enough to let her breathe but kept my hands on her, needing the contact as much as she did.

Thomas spoke next. "I've known you most of my life, Baron. We built our businesses together. Raised our families in the same circles. This isn't you. What happened to our friendship isn't you."

"You don't understand what she's done," said Baron. "The choices she's making. She's throwing her life away on a—"

"You know you're wrong, Baron. Stop this. Now," Tryst interrupted. "She's an adult. She's made her choice, and from where I'm standing, it's a damn good one." My uncle stepped forward and put his hand on Baron's shoulder. The gesture was one of an old friend reaching out to another. "Let it go. Be the *father* she needs."

Baron's expression shifted. The hard mask slipped, and I saw the grief underneath.

Isabel lifted her head. She looked at her father, and I watched her spine straighten.

"You have one chance." She sounded hoarse but certain. "What I told you inside, I meant it."

Baron said nothing.

I took Isabel's hand. "Let's go."

We'd taken two steps when Baron stopped us.

"Wait."

Isabel's grip on my fingers tightened, and she turned around.

"I want to speak with my daughter." His eyes moved to Isabel. "Alone."

Every instinct I had screamed no. After everything he'd done, after the way he'd treated her, leaving her alone with him felt like handing her back to the enemy.

But Isabel squeezed my hand, and when I looked at her, I saw something I hadn't expected. *Confidence.*

"It's okay," she said. "I can do this."

"Isabel—"

"Because of you." She turned to face me fully, her hands coming up to rest on my chest. "I'm strong enough to do this because of you. I already stood up to him before you got here. I said things I've been holding inside my whole life. Whatever he wants to say now, I can handle it."

I searched her face for doubt, for fear, for any sign that she was pushing herself beyond what she could bear.

I found none.

"You're sure?"

"I'm sure."

I cupped her cheeks in my hands and kissed her forehead. "I'll be right here."

She nodded, then walked toward the porch, where her father waited.

I watched her climb the steps to where Baron held the door open, then both of them disappeared inside the house that should have been hers.

I moved to follow.

Tryst's hand closed on my arm. "No."

"I can't—"

"You must." His grip was firm. "You're showing her that you believe in her. That you trust her to fight her own battles."

I stared at the front door, every muscle in my body coiled to move.

Snapper appeared beside me. "He's right."

"I know he's right." I spoke through clenched teeth. "That doesn't make it easier."

"Nothing about loving someone is easy." Snapper began. "But the hardest part isn't fighting for them. It's stepping back when they need to fight for themselves."

The minutes crawled by. Each one felt like an hour.

Bas paced near the SUV, his jaw tight, his eyes flicking to the house every few seconds. Press stood with his arms crossed, watching the windows for any sign of movement. The *Viejos* had moved to a cluster near the circular drive, speaking quietly enough I couldn't hear what they were saying.

I didn't move an inch. I kept my eyes on that door and waited.

My mind constructed a hundred scenarios, each worse than the last. Baron apologizing just long enough to get her guard down. Baron threatening her with something I didn't know about. Baron finding new ways to twist her thoughts until she believed leaving with me was a mistake.

Snapper moved closer, standing shoulder to shoulder with me. He didn't say anything. He didn't need to. His presence was enough—a reminder that I wasn't alone and my family had my back.

Five minutes. Ten. The door stayed closed.

When it finally opened, Isabel stood alone in the doorway.

She looked at me across the distance, and something in her expression made my chest ache. Not pain. Not grief. Peace.

"Kick." She motioned to me. "Come inside."

I hurried up the steps and took her outstretched hand.

Baron's expression was unreadable when he walked past me without speaking. I turned and watched him descend the porch steps toward the *Viejos*, who closed ranks around him. Based on Tryst's body language alone, I was sure they intended a reckoning of their own.

"Where's he going?" I asked.

"To face what's coming, I imagine." She squeezed my fingers. "I'll tell you everything. But not out here."

She led me through the front door.

The foyer was dusty, the crystals of a chandelier overhead clouded with neglect. But beneath the years of abandonment, I could see what this place had been. What it could be again.

"Welcome to Miremont." Isabel's tone was soft. "The only place that felt like home until the day I met you."

I gathered her close and held her. When she finally raised her head, she was smiling through her tears.

"Come on." She took my hand again and led me into what must have been a sitting room. Dust covers draped the furniture, and pale light filtered through grimy windows.

"He told me the truth," she began. "Finally."

I waited, letting her share in her own time.

"Miremont was never sold. It was always mine— left to me by my mother's family. He withheld it, telling himself he was protecting me from my own incompetence." Her laugh was hollow. "He let me grieve this place for five years while it sat here, empty and waiting."

"Jesus, Isabel."

"There's more. My mother's family left me an inheritance. Ten million dollars, held in trust until I turn thirty. I had no idea it existed. He never told me."

Ten million dollars. Hidden from her for years while Baron controlled every aspect of her life, while he threatened to cut her off, while he made her believe she had nothing without him.

"He's releasing it early," she continued. "He has the discretion, apparently. And my trust fund—I'll have control of that as well." She shook her head. "I went from having nothing to having more than I know what to do with in the span of one conversation."

"Why now? What made him do such an about-face?"

"I guess he finally realized he'd lose me for good if he didn't." Her expression shifted. "I think me standing up to him broke something open. Or maybe it was seeing all of you out here, ready to fight for me." She wiped at her cheek. "He said he was sorry. I don't know if I believe him yet. But he's trying. And I told him if he ever tries to control me again, the door closes permanently."

"You're free," I said.

"I'm free." She stepped into my arms, her face pressed against my chest. "And the funny thing is, I don't need any of it anymore. Six months ago, I would have done anything for his approval, for access to that money. Now, I just want you. This life we're building." She looked up at me, and the happiness in her expression made my heart swell. "The rest is just extra."

I kissed her forehead, then her lips.

"Show me our home," I said.

While smaller than Baron's estate, the rooms were more open and spacious. Warmer too. Beneath the dust and neglect, everything was solid—hardwood floors worn smooth by generations of footsteps, window seats built into deep casements with cushions faded but still intact. The kitchen had tile work that looked hand-painted, the colors still vibrant beneath a layer of grime, and a fireplace large enough to cook in.

The air smelled like old wood and dried flowers, with something underneath that might have been lavender. Cobwebs hung in corners, and dust motes floated in the air. But it was all solid. The structure was sound. This was a home that had been waiting, not dying.

"Miremont belonged to my mother's family." Isabel ran her fingers along the wooden surface of a sideboard. "And now, it's mine."

She turned to face me.

"Ours," she said. "If you want it to be."

I looked around the room. "Is this where you want to spend our life together?" I asked.

She held her breath. I could see the hope in her eyes, fragile and fierce at the same time.

"Because I think it's perfect."

The breath rushed out of her, and she laughed and threw her arms around my neck. I lifted her off her feet, spinning her once before setting her down.

"Really?" she asked.

"Really. We can restore it together. Make it ours."

She kissed me, quick and hard, then grabbed my hand again. "There's more. Come on."

We continued through the house. There was a library that was mostly full, but had a few open shelves, and a sunroom with windows on three sides overlooking what must have been gardens once. There were six bedrooms, all on the second floor, each with a fireplace and views of the vineyard hills.

Finally, she led me into an upstairs sitting room near the back. The furniture was draped in white sheets, but above the fireplace hung a portrait that stopped me in my tracks.

The woman in the painting looked out at me with dark eyes and a half smile that made my heart stutter. Her hair was the same color as Isabel's, swept up in a style from another era. She wore a deep-green dress and pearls at her throat. She was beautiful.

"That's you," I breathed.

Isabel squeezed my hand. "That's my grandmother. Anaïs."

I stared at the portrait, at the face that could have been my Isabel's. The resemblance was uncanny. The shape of her eyes. The curve of her mouth. The quiet strength in the set of her shoulders.

Anaïs.

The name settled into my chest and stayed there, warm and certain.

It was perfect for our daughter.

But I didn't say it. Not yet. That moment would come when the time was right, when we knew for certain.

For now, I just stood beside the woman I loved, in the house that would become our home, looking at the face of her grandmother, and held the name close to my heart.

19

Isabel

We continued through the house, room by room, and with each doorway I crossed, the weight on my chest lifted a little more.

Kick held my hand as we climbed the stairs to the second floor. The banister was dusty beneath my free palm, the carpet runner faded and worn, but this house was waiting for someone to bring it back to life. I could feel it.

The first bedroom had a view of how the estate got its name—Miremont's direct translation was "look at the mountain." The second overlooked what had once been a rose garden, now overgrown with wild tangles of thorny branches. The third door stood partially open, and when I pushed it wider, I stopped breathing.

A nursery.

The walls were painted a soft yellow that had aged to cream. A crib stood against one wall, its white spindles dusty but intact. A rocking chair sat near the window, positioned to catch the morning light. Above the crib, someone had painted a vine of delicate flowers that wound across the ceiling, each petal rendered with such care it made my heart swell.

A small dresser stood against the opposite wall, and on top of it, there was a porcelain music box shaped like a carousel.

"Isabel?" Kick said from behind me.

I stepped into the room. My hand found the edge of the crib, and I traced the smooth wood with my fingers. The grain was worn where countless hands must have gripped it during late-night feedings and early-morning risings. A mobile of dancing angels hung above it.

"I've never been in here," I said. "At least not that I remember."

Kick moved to stand beside me. He gazed around the room, then his hand came to rest on my lower back. "Do you think it was your mother's?"

"I do."

He stood behind me, wrapped his arms around my waist, and rested his chin on my shoulder. "Our baby will be so well loved, Isabel. *So* loved."

Something broke open in my chest. I turned into him, pressing my face against his shoulder, and let myself feel the enormity of what was happening. This house. This man. This baby growing inside me. For so long, I had believed I didn't deserve any of it—that wanting too much would only lead to losing everything.

But Kick was here. He hadn't left. And maybe that meant I could finally stop bracing for inevitable pain.

All of this was mine. Ours. But not because it was property, because it was a home.

"Show me the rest," he said against my hair. "I want to see everything."

As the afternoon stretched toward evening, we walked through the vineyards that climbed the gentle slope of the hillside up to the mountain. The vines were dormant and neglected, the trellis wires sagging in places, but I could see what they had been. What they could be again. So could Kick. I knew it without him needing to say so. Resting vines were a luxury few could afford. These had ten years of maturation in them. The fruit they produced would be exquisitely rich, and the wine, magnificent.

"Pinot Noir, mostly," I said as we walked between the rows.

Kick crouched down and examined a gnarled trunk, running his fingers over the bark. "Old vines. Good root systems. They've survived this long without care. With the right attention, they'll produce amazing juice."

I watched him study the vineyard the way a doctor would study a patient—looking for signs of life, assessing what could be saved.

"Did you mean it when you said this place was perfect?" The question came out smaller than I intended.

He stood and turned to face me. The late-afternoon light caught the angles of his face, and I saw nothing but certainty in his eyes.

"I meant it."

"It's a lot of work. Years of it. The house needs everything, and the land—" I gestured at the neglected rows stretching out around us. "Look at it. The winery hasn't been operational in over a decade."

"Isabel." He took my face in his hands. "I grew up in vineyards. My brothers and I have been working harvests since we could walk. There's nothing here that scares me."

"But it's not just the work." I needed him to understand. Needed to be sure this wasn't just adrenaline and relief talking. "It's the commitment. To this place. To me. To building something from nothing when you could go back to Paso Robles and step into a life that's already built."

His thumbs brushed my cheekbones, and his eyes never left mine. "Paso Robles was the place I grew up. Where I became a man. It isn't my home now, Isabel. The two of us here. Making wine. Raising our daughter here"—a smile tugged at the corner of his mouth—"raising a houseful of children, if that's what you want. That's home."

A *houseful*?

"You'd want that?"

"I'd want one child or ten, as long as it's with you."

I kissed him because I couldn't describe what I was feeling. Because the future he was painting was everything I'd been afraid to want. A home. A family. A life built on love instead of obligation.

When we broke apart, I rested my forehead against his. "What about your family? Paso Robles is five hours away. Your mother, your brothers—"

"You're my family now." His gaze bored into mine. "You and our baby. That doesn't mean I love them any less. But my place is with you. Wherever you are."

I raised my head to look at him. "You're sure?"

"I've never been more sure of anything."

We continued to the winery building, a stone structure tucked into the hillside behind the vineyard. The doors were padlocked, with rust blooming around the metal, but we peered through the dusty windows at fermentation tanks, oak barrels, and equipment that had sat unused for too long, waiting for hands that never came.

"It's all here," Kick said, shading his eyes to see better. "It needs to be cleaned, major maintenance, probably some replacement parts. But the infrastructure exists. The bones are good."

"My grandparents made wine here for decades, yet I know so little about it." I pressed my palm against the cool stone wall, feeling the history embedded in it.

"We'll learn it together." Kick's hand covered mine against the stone, his fingers warm where the wall was cold. "We'll bring it back."

I turned to face him. "Promise me something."

"Anything."

"Promise me that if this gets too hard—if the distance from your family becomes too much, or if you start to resent being here—you'll tell me. Don't just pretend everything is fine."

He held my gaze for several seconds. "I promise. But, Isabel, I need you to hear me. *This* is what I want. Since Snapper and I left the rodeo circuit, I haven't been able to figure out what the rest of my life was going to look like. It was as if I was waiting for some kind of sign to point me in the direction I was meant to take." He put his hand on my belly and splayed his fingers. "Turns out it was one *helluva* sign."

By the time we returned to the house, the sun was sinking toward the hills and the driveway stood empty. The men who had come to find me had left hours ago.

Kick squeezed my hand. "What would you like to do? Should we head back to Whitmore?"

"We should."

"You're sure? Will you feel safe there?"

"As long as you're with me—" I stopped myself. "No, that's not right." I put my hands on his chest. "You do make me feel safe, Rascon, but today, I learned that

I can take care of myself too. I faced the person who intimidated me more than any other, and I *won*."

His eyes bored into mine. "What happened when you went back inside with him?"

"Before you arrived, I gave him an ultimatum. Actually, first, I said everything I'd held inside all my life. When he asked to speak with me, I had nothing left to say, but I was ready to listen. If I told anyone else what he said, it wouldn't sound like much, but to me, it was everything. Everything I needed. Including to tell me that Miremont had always been mine and how sorry he was to have kept it from me."

Kick nodded, and I got it would be hard for him to understand, especially with how demonstrative his family was. But I didn't expect that of Baron—of my father—it was all he was capable of.

The drive to Whitmore was quiet. I watched the landscape roll past, lit by moonlight—vineyard after vineyard, hills giving way to valleys and rising again. My hand rested on my stomach, and I felt the baby shift beneath my palm. A flutter, nothing more. But real. Alive. Ours.

When we arrived at the Whitmore estate, Thomas was standing on the porch. Bas paced beside him, his body tight with tension, and the moment our car came into view, he stopped moving. His hands dropped to his sides. Even from a distance, I could see him exhale.

I barely had the door open before he was there, crossing the distance in long strides and gathering me into a hug that was brief but fierce. His arms tightened around me, and I felt a tremor run through him—something that might have been fear finally releasing its grip.

"Don't ever do that again," he said against my hair. "Don't ever disappear like that."

"I didn't have a choice."

"I know." He leaned away, his hands still on my shoulders, and I saw something in his face I'd never noticed before. Something raw and unguarded, something that looked almost like grief. His eyes searched mine with an intensity that made my breath catch.

Then his jaw tightened, and whatever I'd glimpsed was gone, shuttered behind the easy smile I'd known since childhood.

Then I felt Kick's arm snake around my waist.

Bas looked over my shoulder at him, back at me, then he stepped away, putting distance between us that felt deliberate.

"Thank God you're safe." Thomas descended the porch steps and embraced me with the gentleness of a father.

"I'm fine. I'm more than fine." Kick moved to stand beside me. "We have a lot to tell you."

Thomas led us inside, and we gathered in his study—the same room where he'd offered me a job what felt like a lifetime ago. Bas stood near the window, arms crossed, while Thomas settled into his chair behind the desk.

"I understand Miremont is yours?" he began.

"It is, and we want to restore it. The house, the vineyards, the winery. All of it," I told him.

"That's a significant undertaking."

"We know." Kick's hand found mine. "But we're not planning to abandon Whitmore. We want to stay through this year's harvest. Help with everything we committed to, the initiatives we've been developing. We have a presentation ready whenever you want to see it."

Thomas was quiet for a moment, his fingers steepled beneath his chin. Then he looked at his son.

"What do you think, Sebastian?"

Bas blinked. "What do you mean?"

"No time like the present, I suppose." Thomas began. "I'm retiring. Stepping back from day-to-day operations. Whitmore is yours now—it has been for a while, really. I've just been too stubborn to make it official."

The silence that followed was heavy with surprise. Bas stared at his father, his composure cracking for the first time since we'd arrived.

"You're serious."

"I'm sixty-three years old, and I'm tired." Thomas smiled. "You've been running this place better than I have for years. It's time I stopped pretending otherwise."

Bas turned to look at me, then at Kick. The raw expression I'd glimpsed earlier flickered across his face again before he steeled his expression.

"Then, I hope we can work together," he said. "All of us. Whitmore and Miremont."

"We'd like that," I said. And I meant it. Bas had been my friend since childhood, and whatever complicated feelings might be lurking beneath the surface, our partnership would work. I didn't doubt it.

Thomas's phone buzzed. He glanced at the screen, and surprise flickered across his face.

"Everything okay?" Bas asked.

"That was your father," Thomas said, looking at me. "He's asked if we might meet and talk through some things."

Kick's hand tightened on mine.

"How did you respond?" I asked.

"Baron—your father—and I were friends for thirty years before our falling out. Good friends. I'm not saying I've forgiven what he did to you—that's not mine to forgive. But if he's genuinely trying to make amends…" He shrugged. "I suppose I'm willing to hear him out."

I nodded slowly. "That's between the two of you."

"It is." Thomas held my gaze. "But I wanted you to know."

"Thank you," I said.

"It's been a long day for everyone. You two should rest. We can talk more tomorrow."

My body ached with exhaustion I hadn't let myself feel until now. The adrenaline that had carried me through the confrontation, the tour, and the drive back—all of it was fading, leaving only bone-deep weariness behind.

"Thank you again," I said to Thomas. "For everything."

"You're family, Isabel. Both of you." He glanced at Kick. "Take care of her."

"Always."

20

Kick

Baron Van Orr had stood before Los Caballeros three nights ago, and I still couldn't quite believe what I'd witnessed.

He'd come to our meeting room in the wine cave at Tryst's request—a summons, really, though it had been phrased as an invitation. The *Viejos* had gathered in full, along with the current members—my generation.

I'd expected defiance when he stood before us. Maybe another attempt at justification for what he'd done.

Instead, the man who faced his fellow *caballeros* was better described as broken. Humbled.

"I have no excuse for what I did," Baron began, his delivery stripped of its usual polish. "I told myself I was protecting my daughter. That I knew what was best for her. But the truth is, I was trying to control her the way I've controlled everything else in my life." He paused. "I kidnapped my own child. I tried to take her baby from her. I don't know how to live with that."

The silence in the room was absolute.

"I understand if you intend to remove me from Los Caballeros. But I'm asking—" His voice cracked. "I'm asking for the chance to make amends. Not just to Isabel, but to all of you. To this brotherhood I've dishonored."

After Tryst asked Baron to step outside, the debate that ensued was heated. Some said what he'd done was unforgivable, a betrayal of everything we stood for. Others argued for mercy.

"Who among us hasn't done something we regret?" Tryst asked. "Something we'd give anything to take back?"

"All of us have," Michael Barrett responded, and when he looked at each of us seated around him, everyone nodded. Myself included.

I hadn't spoken. It didn't feel right to. But if I had been asked, I would've said to let him stay. And in the end, that's how we voted.

However, there were terms. If Baron ever interfered in Isabel's life again, if he ever tried to control or manipulate her, the evidence the *caballeros* had gathered would go to law enforcement and he'd not be welcome in Los Caballeros ever again.

Baron had accepted the terms without argument. He'd thanked us and left the cave, looking like a man who'd been given a second chance he wasn't sure he deserved.

I couldn't say that I'd forgiven him. I wasn't sure I ever would completely. But watching him humble himself before the brotherhood, watching him finally take responsibility for the damage he'd caused—it was a start. And for Isabel's sake, I'd welcome him to be a part of our lives in whatever way she wanted him to be.

Now, Isabel stood at the head of the table in Thomas Whitmore's study, and I couldn't take my eyes off her.

She'd been preparing for this presentation for weeks, refining the pitch until every slide was polished, every talking point sharpened to a fine edge. The 1934 Society had started as her idea—a membership program that would bring Whitmore's most loyal customers into an exclusive circle, offering them access to limited releases, private tastings, and behind-the-scenes experiences that money alone couldn't buy.

Now, she was selling it, and she was magnificent.

"The wine industry is changing," she said, advancing to the next slide. "Customers don't just want a bottle anymore. They want a story. They want to feel like they're part of something. The 1934 Society gives them that connection."

Thomas shifted in his chair, his attention fixed on the screen. Bas sat beside him, arms crossed, but his expression was engaged rather than skeptical.

Isabel walked them through the tiers—the pricing structure, the benefits at each level, the projected enrollment numbers, based on Whitmore's existing customer database. She answered questions without hesitation, pivoting when Thomas raised concerns about staffing, addressing Bas' question about event logistics with specifics she'd clearly thought through in advance.

She was in her element. Confident. Capable. Brilliant.

When she finished, the room was quiet for a moment. Thomas' expression was unreadable.

Then he smiled.

"This is exactly what we needed," he said. "Better than I hoped. Isabel, this is exceptional work."

Her face lit up. The change was subtle—a softening around her eyes, a lift at the corners of her mouth—but I saw it.

I wanted to cross the room and pull her into my arms. Instead, I caught her eye and let my expression communicate what I couldn't say in front of everyone else.

I'm proud of you.

She ducked her head, but not before I saw her smile widen.

"I think this calls for a celebration," Thomas said, pushing back from the table. "Bas, grab that bottle we've been saving."

We moved from the study to the living room, where the afternoon light filtered through tall windows and cast long shadows across the hardwood floor. Bas returned with a bottle of Whitmore's reserve Pinot Noir and poured some for everyone except Isabel, who accepted sparkling water with a grace that had become second nature.

"To the 1934 Society," Thomas raised his glass. "And to the team who created it."

We drank. Isabel's cheeks flushed pink, and she leaned into my side when I slipped my arm around her waist.

"I've been doing some research," Bas said, swirling his wine. "Isabel, are you aware that Miremont's first bottling was in 1934?"

She blinked. "I had no idea."

Bas exchanged a glance with his father. "What if we created the society together? Combined our histories—Whitmore with Miremont."

"That's a great idea. There are several other wineries in the valley that were either founded then or reinvented themselves after the end of Prohibition," Thomas added. "I'm sure they'd want to be part of something like this."

I watched Isabel process the suggestion, witnessed her mind work through the implications. A society that spanned multiple wineries. A collaboration that could put Miremont on the map before we'd even produced our first vintage.

"It could work," she said slowly. "We'd need to restructure some of the membership tiers, create a framework that allows each winery to maintain its identity while sharing the benefits of the collective brand."

"That's why you're the marketing director," Bas said with a grin. "We just throw out ideas. You figure out how to turn them into something viable."

The conversation continued, but I found my attention drifting. To Isabel, animated and engaged. To the ring hidden in my pocket. To the question I'd been rehearsing for weeks, waiting for the right moment to ask.

After the meeting wound down and we'd said our goodbyes, I drove back to Miremont alone. Isabel and Bas had a meeting with one of Whitmore's distributors that would keep her occupied for another few hours, which gave me time to think.

The house restoration was coming along faster than anticipated. The renovation crew, made up of current *caballeros* and *Viejos*, had finished the kitchen last week, and the master bedroom was nearly complete. The nursery—that soft yellow room with the painted vines—had been cleaned, the artwork restored, and the old crib replaced with a new one that met modern safety standards. Every day, it looked a little more like a home.

I walked into the sitting room where the portrait of Anaïs hung and took the velvet box from my pocket.

The ring inside had belonged to my grandmother on my mother's side. It was a simple gold band with a single diamond that caught the light and threw tiny rainbows across my palm. My mother had given it to me a few weeks ago, pressing it into my hand with tears in her eyes.

"Your *abuela* wore this for sixty-two years," she'd said. "It brought her joy. Let it bring Isabel the same."

I'd been waiting for the perfect moment to give it to her. To first find the ideal setting that would make the proposal worthy of the woman I wanted to spend my life with.

I'd imagined a dozen scenarios. A sunset over the vineyard. A private dinner in the newly restored dining room. A trip back to that bar in Paso Robles where everything had started between us. Each idea seemed right for a moment, then wrong the next. Too staged. Too predictable. Too *perfected*.

But maybe perfect wasn't the point. Maybe real was.

I closed the box and held it in my palm, feeling the weight of everything it represented. A promise. A future. A commitment that went beyond words.

The sound of trucks in the driveway brought me back to the present. I tucked the ring in my pocket and went downstairs.

Snapper's SUV was parked near the winery building, and behind it came Bit's, towing a flatbed loaded with equipment.

"About time you showed your face," Bit called out as I crossed the yard. "Where've you been?"

"Contemplating my existence," I shot back. "Deep philosophical stuff. Shit you wouldn't understand."

"Philosophy." Bit snorted. "Is that what they're calling it now?"

Snapper appeared from around the side of the flatbed, wiping his hands on his jeans. "He was staring at that ring again. I can tell by the look on his face."

"I was not."

"You were." He grinned. "Just ask her already."

Bit stood near his truck, arms folded across his chest. "What's the holdup, little brother? Cold feet?"

"No." I grabbed a toolbox from the flatbed, more to give my hands something to do than because I needed it. "I want it to be right."

"It's Isabel." Snapper fell into step beside me as we walked toward the winery. "You're having a baby together. You're building a life here. What could be more right than that?"

"I want the moment to be special."

"Special how? You planning to hire a mariachi band? Skywrite her name? Rent out a stadium?"

"No, I just—" I set down the toolbox and turned to face him. "I want her to know how much I love her. Not just the baby. Her."

Snapper's teasing expression softened. "She knows you do. There's no doubt." He gazed off in the distance. "I get it. You wait for the right moment. Try to make a plan. Then the woman you love shows up Christmas morning at dawn, and you sink to your knees because you know that is not just the right moment. It's the only moment." He held my gaze. "All you need to be is sure. Are you?"

"I've never been more certain of anything."

"Then, stop overthinking it. It doesn't have to be perfect. She just needs to hear how you feel, and she needs to believe it. That's all."

We spent the afternoon working on the winery building, cleaning the equipment, replacing rusted fittings, and assessing what could be salvaged and what needed to go. My brothers gave me grief about everything from my technique with a wrench to the color Isabel had chosen for the tasting room walls, and by the time the sun started sinking toward the hills, my muscles ached and my mind was quiet.

This was what I needed. Physical work. My brothers' company. The reminder that I wasn't building this life alone.

Isabel texted as they were loading up to leave. *Heading home. See you in an hour.*

Home. She called it home now. It meant more than she probably knew.

I showered and changed, then sat on the edge of the bed and took out the ring one more time. The diamond caught the fading light, and I turned it between my fingers.

Tonight, I thought. And then pushed the thought away.

We had the anatomy scan in the morning. The appointment where we'd finally see our baby in detail and confirm that everything was developing the way it should. That felt like the moment to focus on first.

The ring could wait one more day.

Isabel lay on the examination table in the doctor's office, wearing a gown that opened in the front while I held her hand and tried to look calmer than I felt.

Isabel's fingers tightened on mine. She was nervous too, I realized. Hiding it better than I was, but nervous.

"You know the drill, this might be a little cold," the doctor warned before squeezing gel onto Isabel's skin.

She flinched, then laughed. "It feels like you kept it in the freezer."

The doctor laughed too, then moved the wand across her stomach. The screen flickered to life and shapes emerged from the static—curves and shadows that slowly morphed into something recognizable.

A head. A spine. Tiny hands with fingers I could count. Feet that kicked and flexed as we watched.

"There's your baby," she said, adjusting the angle. "Let me just take some measurements."

I stared at the screen, unable to look away. The last ultrasound had shown a blob, barely human-shaped, a grainy image that required imagination to interpret. This was different. This was a person. A tiny, perfect person with a nose and lips and a heartbeat I could see pulsing on the monitor. She was moving, stretching, living inside the woman I loved.

The doctor worked in silence for several minutes, clicking, measuring, and typing notes I couldn't read. Each pause made my heart rate spike, but her expression remained calm, professional, and reassuring.

"Everything looks great," she finally said. "Growth is right on track. Strong heartbeat. Good movement. Brain development is normal. The heart has four chambers, all functioning properly. Spine is intact. Kidneys, stomach, bladder—all present and accounted for."

The relief that washed through me was physical, a loosening of tension I hadn't realized I carried. Isabel let out a breath that sounded like she'd been holding it since we walked in.

"Do you want to know the sex?"

We'd discussed this. We'd said we wanted to know, wanted to be prepared, wanted to stop assuming we were having a girl and be sure. Maybe even start talking about names. But now that the moment was here, I felt my heart slam against my ribs.

Isabel looked at me. I nodded.

"Yes," she said. "We want to know."

The wand moved, and we studied the screen.

"It's a girl."

A chill went through me. I'd known—we'd both known—in that instinctive way that defied logic, but hearing it confirmed made it real. Our daughter. Our little girl. The baby who would sleep in that yellow nursery, who would grow up running through the vineyard rows, who would inherit Isabel's dark eyes and—God willing—her strength.

My vision blurred. I blinked hard, but the tears came anyway.

"Rascon?" Isabel said softly.

I brought her hand to my lips and pressed a kiss against her knuckles. "I'm fine," I managed. "I'm better than fine."

In the car afterward, we sat in the parking lot without starting the engine. Isabel stared through the windshield, one hand resting on her belly.

"We're having a girl," she said.

"We knew."

She turned to look at me. "We did." Her smile was so broad that the sight of it cracked something open in my chest. I'd never imagined the happiness I felt existed.

I started the car and drove out of the parking lot. The ring was waiting at home, hidden in a drawer, patient as it had been for weeks.

But I was done waiting.

21

Isabel

A girl.

I couldn't stop thinking about it as we drove back to Miremont. The image from the ultrasound was burned into my memory—that tiny profile, the curve of her nose, the way she'd stretched and kicked as if already impatient to meet the world.

Our daughter.

Kick's hand found mine on the center console, and I laced my fingers through his. Neither of us spoke. We didn't need to. The joy filling the car was tangible, warm, and enough.

When we arrived at the house, the last of the afternoon light was fading behind the hills. Home. It still gave me a small thrill to think of it that way—this place that had been abandoned and forgotten, now filled with life again. Our life.

Inside, Kick disappeared into the kitchen while I went upstairs and wandered into the sitting room.

Someone—probably Kick—had already laid fresh wood in the grate, ready to be lit.

"Dinner's almost ready," Kick called up to me.

"You made dinner?" I asked, walking out and looking down on him from the landing.

"Come eat."

I joined him to find the table set with mismatched plates and candles stuck in empty wine bottles. The meal was simple—roasted chicken, potatoes, and a salad made from greens I suspected came from Whitmore's garden. Nothing fancy. But the effort he'd put into it made my chest ache.

"This looks so good!"

"Don't sound so surprised." He pulled out my chair with exaggerated formality. "I have hidden depths."

"Clearly."

We ate by candlelight, talking about nothing in particular. The renovation progress. Whether we should get a dog once we were settled or wait until after the baby was born. Easy conversation, the kind that came from knowing someone so well that silence wasn't uncomfortable.

But something was off.

Kick kept fidgeting. Adjusting his napkin. Reaching for his water glass, then setting it down without drinking. His knee bounced under the table, a nervous habit I'd never seen from him before.

"Are you okay?" I asked.

"Fine," he said too quickly.

I raised a brow but didn't push.

After dinner, we returned to the sitting room, where he lit a fire in the grate. The warmth of it filled the space as my grandmother looked down from her portrait with a serene expression, as if she approved of what was happening in her house.

I settled onto the sofa, and Kick sat beside me. Close, but not touching. His hands clasped between his knees, his gaze fixed on the flames.

"You're being weird," I said.

He glanced at me. "Weird?"

"Not bad weird. Just…" I studied his face, the tension around his eyes, the set of his jaw. "Something's going on. You've been jumpy all through dinner."

He laughed, but it sounded strained. "That obvious?"

"To me? Yes."

The fire popped and hissed in the silence that followed. Outside, the wind moved through the vineyard, rustling the bare vines.

Then he turned to face me fully, and the look in his eyes made my heart stutter.

"I've been trying to figure out the right way to do this," he said. "The right words. The right moment. I've been carrying this around for weeks, waiting for some perfect opportunity that probably doesn't exist."

"Carrying what?"

He reached into his pocket and took out a small velvet box.

My breath caught.

"Isabel." He sounded steadier, the nervousness replaced by something deeper. He shifted off the sofa and got on one knee. "You're the only person I can imagine my life with. I fell in love with you in that bar two years ago. I just didn't know it yet."

He opened the box. Inside, a ring gleamed in the firelight.

"This was my grandmother's," he said. "Lucia's mother."

Tears blurred my vision. I blinked them back, not wanting to miss a single moment of this.

Kick took the ring from the box and lifted my left hand. "Isabel Van Orr, will you marry me?"

His proposal landed in my chest and bloomed there, filling every hollow space I'd ever carried. This man. This life. This future stretching out before us, full of possibilities I'd never dared to imagine.

"You showed up and refused to leave." My voice broke. "You made me believe I was worth staying for."

"Is that a yes?"

"*Yes.*" I laughed through the tears streaming down my face. "Yes, of course yes."

He slid the ring onto my finger. It fit perfectly, as if it had been made for me.

Then he pulled me off the sofa and into his arms, and I kissed him with everything I had. Joy and relief and love so fierce it almost hurt. He held me tight, one hand cradling the back of my head, the other splayed across my lower back, and I felt our daughter kick between us—as if she knew something important had just happened.

"Hey there, little one," he said, resting his hand on my belly. His eyes widened when she kicked again. "I guess you approve."

When we finally broke apart, we were both laughing. Crying a little too. The kind of messy, happy tears that came from getting everything you'd ever wanted.

"We should call your mother," I said.

"She's going to lose her mind."

"I know. That's why we should call her first."

He grabbed his phone from the coffee table and dialed. I pressed close to his side so I could hear, his arm wrapped around me, my left hand resting on his chest where I could see the ring catch the firelight.

Lucia answered on the second ring. "*Mijo?* Is everything okay?"

"Everything's perfect, Ma. Isabel and I have news."

"What kind of news?"

Kick looked at me, his eyes bright. "She said yes."

The shriek that came through the phone made us both wince and laugh. I could hear Lucia crying, words tumbling out in a mix of English and Spanish too fast to follow.

"My baby," she finally managed. "My last baby, getting married. Oh, *mijo*. Your father would be so proud. He would be so, so proud."

I thought of Kick's father, the man whose presence I felt in every story his children told. The patriarch who had built this family, whose legacy lived on in his sons and daughter.

"Thank you, Lucia," I said, leaning toward the phone. "For raising him. For welcoming me."

"*Mija,* you are my daughter. You always will be."

We talked for a few more minutes—about the ring, about the proposal, about when we might have a wedding—then Lucia insisted we call the rest of the family before they heard the news from someone else.

Snapper answered on the first ring. "Tell me you finally did it."

Brix offered quiet congratulations and said he looked forward to welcoming me officially. Bit made a joke about Kick finally growing up, then said how happy he was for us. Cru said he supposed Snapper would be the best man, even though he should be, since he'd named him.

"What do you mean?" Kick asked.

"Rascon. It was my idea."

"I've never heard that story before."

Cru laughed. "That's because it isn't true. I just thought maybe it would get me the best-man gig. I'll settle for groomsman, though. Unless you want me to officiate."

"Are you ordained?" I asked.

"No, but I think you can do it in like a day."

We both laughed, and Kick ended the call, saying he had to tell Alex before she heard it from someone else.

His sister squealed so loud that he held the phone away from his ear. "I knew it," she said. "I knew you two were perfect for each other. I called it years ago."

"You did not," Kick said.

"I absolutely did. Ask anyone."

By the time we'd made it through the family, my face hurt from smiling. We collapsed onto the sofa, tangled together, the fire burning low in the grate.

"That was a lot," I said.

"Welcome to the Avilas." Kick pressed a kiss to my temple. "It only gets bigger and louder from here."

I smiled and nestled closer. His hand found my belly, resting there the way it always did now, as if he couldn't stop reaching for our daughter.

"Have you thought of any names?" he asked.

"I have." I hesitated. "But I'm not sure you'll like it."

"It?" He tilted his head to look at me. "Just one?"

"Just one."

"Tell me."

"Anaïs."

He closed his eyes, and a smile spread across his face, slow and certain, like sunrise breaking over the vineyard hills.

"I thought of one too. Just one," he said. When he opened his eyes, they were bright with emotion. *"Anaïs."*

My breath caught. "You—"

"The moment I saw her face. Your grandmother's face. Your face." He cupped my cheek in his palm. "I've been holding onto that name for weeks, waiting for the right time to say it."

"Anaïs Avila," I whispered.

"Perfect," he said. "Just like her mother."

I kissed him, soft and slow, tasting the future on his lips.

"She's going to grow up with so much love," I said when we finally broke apart. "Grandparents, aunts, uncles, cousins. All those people who just screamed at us through the phone."

"Chaos," he agreed.

"The best kind."

We lay there, in the quiet, the fire crackling softly, the ring warm on my finger. Outside, the vineyard stretched, dark and dormant, waiting for spring. Inside, everything was warmth and light, with the steady rhythm of Kick's heartbeat beneath my ear.

This was my life now. This man. This family. This house that we would fill with children and laughter and wine made from grapes we'd grown ourselves.

I closed my eyes and let myself believe it.

All of it. Finally.

22

Kick

"Rascon?"

I blinked in the darkness, disoriented, reaching for her before I was fully awake.

Her hand found my arm, fingers pressing hard. "It's time."

The statement hit me like ice water. I sat up, heart hammering, every thought scattering in different directions at once.

"Now? Are you sure? How far apart are the—"

"I'm sure." Her voice was strained but steady. "My water broke. We need to go."

I threw off the covers and promptly tripped over my own shoes, cursed, and found the light switch. Isabel was already sitting up, one hand pressed to her belly, her face tight with concentration.

"Okay." I took a breath, then another, forcing myself to think. "Okay. Hospital bag is by the door. Car keys are on the hook. I'll bring the car around."

"Rascon."

I stopped halfway to the closet.

"Pants," she said. "You might want pants."

I looked down at my boxers. Right. Pants.

Three minutes later, we were in the car.

It's time. Heading to hospital now, I texted Snapper, who, along with most of the rest of my family, had been staying in one of several guest houses on Press' estate. They'd arrived two days ago after Ma insisted the baby would come before the end of the week.

His response came before we hit the main road. *On our way. Don't let her have that baby without us.*

"Right," I muttered. Somehow, I doubted it was up to Isabel or me. Our daughter, our precious Anaïs, would come into this world in her own time. She'd learned well from her mother.

The drive to the hospital was a blur of dark roads and Isabel's controlled breathing. I held her hand at every red light, watching her face in the glow of the dashboard, counting the seconds between contractions.

"You're doing great," I told her.

"You're speeding."

"Only a little."

By the time we reached the hospital and got Isabel settled into a room, the first wave of reinforcements had arrived. My mother burst through the waiting room doors less than an hour after my text, still in her travel clothes, her eyes wild with excitement.

"How far along? Where's the doctor? Get the doctor. She needs to be here. Now."

"Jeez, Ma, Isabel is in *labor*. You've done it enough times to know they're monitoring her, but it's going to be a while."

"A while." She grabbed my face in both hands and kissed my forehead. "My baby is having a baby. I can't believe it."

Alex and Maddox arrived next, then Snapper and Saffron, followed by Bit and Eberly, then Cru and Daphne, then Brix and Addison. The waiting room filled with Avilas, whose presence turned the sterile space into something that felt almost like home.

"Who's watching the kids?" I asked when I realized none had come along.

"Baron," quipped Alex.

"No!"

She laughed. "Hell, no. Laird and Sorcha have been camped out on Ma's doorstep since Isabel's due date came and went."

Maddox's mother and father were probably the only people on earth our mother would trust with her "g-babies," as she called them.

I returned to Isabel's room, holding her hand through contractions that came harder and faster as the hours passed. Every few minutes, a different woman would come to check on her progress. Finally, Isabel asked Alex if she'd get to Lucia and if they would both mind staying. While most women probably would've touched their heart, moved by the request, my sister whooped her way back to the waiting room.

"Your family is insane," Isabel whispered after she left. The lull was brief, and within seconds, her grip on my fingers was strong enough to leave bruises.

"Our family," I corrected, stroking her damp hair and feeding her a spoonful of ice chips.

She laughed, then winced as another contraction started to build. "Our family. God help us."

Alex returned, dragging our mother behind her. And miraculously, their presence seemed to calm Isabel.

The labor stretched through the night and into the morning. I lost track of time, lost track of everything except her and the monitors and the nurses who came and went with calm efficiency. She was exhausted. I was terrified. But every time I looked at her face, I saw the same determination that had carried her through everything else.

And then, finally, the doctor said the words I'd been waiting for.

"One more push."

Isabel bore down, her hand crushing mine, a sound tearing from her throat that was half scream and half triumph. And then—a cry. Thin and furious and absolutely perfect.

"Welcome, baby girl," the doctor said, placing her on Isabel's chest after cutting the umbilical cord. She'd asked me if I wanted to, then reneged when I felt the room start to spin.

The tiny, squalling, red-faced creature who had turned our lives upside down before she'd even taken her first breath rested on her mother's chest, staring up at her as if to say hello. Isabel's arms came up to cradle her, instinctive and sure, and her face crumpled.

"She's perfect," she whispered. "Rascon, look at her. She's perfect."

I couldn't speak. My throat had closed up, my vision blurred with tears I didn't bother to hide. I leaned down and pressed my forehead to Isabel's, one hand cupping the back of our daughter's impossibly small head.

"Welcome to the world, Anaïs," I managed.

Isabel nodded, tears streaming down her cheeks. "Anaïs."

Alex and Ma crowded on Isabel's other side, gazing down at the newest member of our family. Tears streaked down both their cheeks, which only made mine fall harder.

The nurse took our baby girl briefly to clean her up, check her vitals, and wrap her in a soft pink blanket. When they returned, they placed her in my arms.

I looked down at my daughter's face. Her eyes were closed, her tiny fists curled against her cheeks. She had a dusting of dark hair and a rosebud mouth that pursed and relaxed as she slept.

"Hey, baby girl." I said, choking back tears. "I'm your papa. I've been talking to you for months. Nice to finally meet you."

She yawned. The smallest, most devastating yawn I'd ever seen.

I was gone. Completely, utterly gone.

Alex left the room, asking who else she could send in. Isabel answered "*everyone*" before I could say they could all wait. Ma, though, wouldn't leave. She took Anaïs from my arms with the practiced ease of a woman who had raised seven children, and held her close.

"She looks like you, Rascon." A tear ran down her cheek. "When you were born. The same face. Alfonso would have—" She couldn't finish. Just shook her head and held our daughter like the precious thing she was.

Snapper came next, with Saffron, then brothers and sisters-in-law in a parade of happy tears and whispered congratulations. Anaïs was examined and adored and declared the most beautiful baby any of them had ever seen—other than their own.

I watched Isabel through all of it. Watched her accept the embraces, the kisses, the overwhelming flood of love from people who hadn't truly known her less than a year ago. She didn't hesitate. Didn't retreat behind the walls she'd spent so long building.

She let them love her.

When the room finally emptied and the door clicked shut behind my mother, who Alex finally convinced to give us time on our own, the silence felt like a gift. Isabel lay propped against the pillows, with Anaïs asleep in her arms. I sank into the chair by the bed and reached for her hand.

"You did it," I said.

"We did it." She turned her head to look at our daughter, and her smile was tired but radiant. "She's beautiful."

"And perfect."

When she handed her to me, I settled into the chair with her cradled against my chest. Her tiny body felt so warm and solid in my arms. She stirred but didn't wake.

"She looks nothing like me," I said, studying her face. "She looks just like you."

Isabel laughed softly. "Give her time. She might grow into your nose."

"God, I hope not."

We sat in comfortable silence, the three of us, while the hospital hummed quietly around us. I thought about everything that had led to this moment. The months of uncertainty and fear and slowly building trust.

"We made her," I said, still not quite believing it. "You and me."

"We did." Isabel's eyes met mine across the dim room. "Thank you for not giving up on me," she added quietly.

I kissed her forehead, then her lips, soft and slow. "Never."

Epilogue

Isabel

The Avila women had taken over the master bedroom at Miremont.

Alex was doing my makeup while Saffron fussed with my hair. Eberly had commandeered the steamer and was attacking invisible wrinkles in my dress. Daphne was entertaining Anaïs on the bed, making ridiculous faces that had my daughter gurgling with laughter.

Four months old, and she already had everyone wrapped around her tiny fingers.

"Hold still," Alex ordered, brandishing a mascara wand. "You're going to end up looking like a raccoon."

"I'm nervous," I bit back, which made Alex smile and look at me like she was a proud mama herself.

"You're marrying my brother. You should be nervous. You're stuck with us forever now."

I laughed, and she sighed and waited for me to stop moving before finishing my eyes.

This was my life now. Chaos and laughter and women who had absorbed me into their ranks without question. I hadn't known what it meant to be surrounded by people who showed up, who helped, who made your problems their problems without being asked.

I knew now.

The door opened, and Lucia stepped inside. She wore a deep-burgundy dress that set off her silver hair, and her eyes went bright the moment she saw me.

"Oh, *mija*." Her hand pressed to her heart. "You're beautiful."

I stood, careful not to step on the hem of my dress, and turned to face her. The gown was simple—ivory silk, clean lines, and a neckline that skimmed my collarbones. No beading, no lace, no elaborate train. Just me.

"Thank you." I crossed the room and took her hands in mine. "For everything. For loving me, most of all."

Lucia's eyes filled with tears. She cupped my face the way she always cupped her children's faces, like I was precious.

"That's what mothers do," she said.

I hugged her, and she held me tight, and when we finally separated, we were both laughing at ourselves for crying before the ceremony had even started.

"Enough!" Alex declared. "I am not fixing that makeup again. Everyone, pull yourselves together."

The ceremony was held in the rose garden that Rascon and I had painstakingly brought back to what I imagined was its former glory. Eberly, who had the greenest thumb of anyone I knew, probably deserved the most credit.

We'd set up rows of chairs, with an arbor at the end, draped in white flowers and trailing greenery. The November sun hung golden in the sky, casting long shadows across the hills.

I stood at the entrance to the aisle, alone.

My father had asked to do the honors, but I'd gently told him no. Not out of anger, though. As I'd explained to him, this moment was *mine*. Today, I would give *myself* to the man I loved.

The music started. I took a breath and stepped forward.

Every face turned toward me. Friends and family, colleagues and neighbors, people who had become part of my life in ways I never could have predicted.

I saw Thomas in the front row, his smile warm with approval. I saw Bas standing beside him, his eyes suspiciously bright.

I scanned the crowd for one more face.

On Thomas' opposite side, on the aisle, stood my father. Our eyes met across the distance, and he nodded and smiled.

I smiled back, then turned my attention to the flower-draped arbor, where Rascon waited with a smile so wide it looked like it might split his face. He wore a charcoal suit with an ivory tie, and he'd never looked more handsome.

I reached him, and he took my hands, and Cru began to speak. Yes, he'd become ordained so he could marry us. I heard maybe half of what he said. The rest was lost to the rush of blood in my ears, the pounding of my heart, the overwhelming awareness of the man standing in front of me.

Then it was time for the vows.

Kick went first. He cleared his throat and squeezed my hands.

"Isabel. You taught me that love isn't about rescuing someone. It's about showing up. Every day. In the small moments and the hard ones. In the middle of the night when the baby won't stop crying and in the morning when the coffee's not ready. I promise to show up for you. Every day. For the rest of my life."

It was my turn to say what I'd written and rewritten a dozen times, but standing here, looking at his face, they came easy.

"Rascon, I spent my life running. From expectations, from disappointment, from anything that felt too much like hope. You're the reason I finally stopped. Not because you caught me—but because you made me want to stay. I promise to stay. With you. With our daughter. With this life we're building together. Forever."

Cru pronounced us husband and wife. Kick kissed me, and the crowd erupted, and somewhere behind us, Anaïs let out a delighted shriek that made everyone laugh.

The reception was ongoing chaos in the best possible way.

Tables had been set up beneath a tent on the lawn behind the house. Lights that would glow like stars once the sun went down were strung inside. Music played from speakers hidden in the garden, and the wine flowed freely—Whitmore and Avila vintages side by side. Soon, Miremont would be poured, maybe in time for the next wedding.

Anaïs was passed from aunt to uncle like a tiny celebrity, accepting adoration with the regal disinterest of someone who knew she was the most important person in the room. When she finally got fussy, Lucia swept her away for a bottle and a nap, and I was free to circulate.

I found myself near the bar when I noticed Bas.

He was talking to Gemma Engel, our wedding planner. She looked polished and professional with her dark hair swept back in a sleek chignon and a headset hooked over one ear even now. She'd been putting out fires all day—literally, when one of the candles had gotten too close to a centerpiece—and she looked like she was running on caffeine and sheer willpower.

Bas had turned on the charm. I could see it from twenty feet away—the easy smile, the relaxed posture, the way he got just close enough to create intimacy without crowding her. It was his standard move. I'd seen it work on countless women over the years.

But it wasn't working on Gemma.

She said something polite but firm, then she excused herself and walked away, already speaking into her headset about something involving the cake.

The expression on Bas' face made me pause as he watched her go.

"Interesting," I murmured.

Alex appeared at my elbow, following my gaze. "Poor Bas. Shot down in flames."

"I doubt it happens often."

"You're right." Alex grinned. "And it might be good for him." She leaned closer. "I've been thinking. Now that you're settled here, we should start a Wicked Winemakers Ball for the Russian River Valley. Raise money for the children's hospital, the way we do in Paso Robles."

"That's a great idea."

"I know. And I already have someone in mind to organize it."

I held up my hands. "Oh no. Not me. I have a vineyard to restore and a baby to raise and—"

Alex laughed. "I hope I don't hurt your feelings, but I wasn't thinking of you." She nodded toward Gemma, who was now directing the catering staff while making sure the cake was ready to cut. "She'd be perfect."

"You're right. If she'll do it."

Alex cocked her head. "Oh, my dear sister-in-law. You know me. *She'll do it.*"

The evening wound down in a haze of champagne and dancing and more happiness than I'd ever thought possible. When Rascon found me on the dance floor and put his arms around me, I melted into him without hesitation.

"Did you see Bas with the wedding planner?" I asked.

"I saw." His hand spread warm across my lower back. "He's had that look all night."

"What look?"

His eyes met mine. "The one I had when I finally stopped pretending I wasn't in love with you."

I laughed and kissed him, and we swayed together until the song ended.

Later—much later—we stood alone on the patio. The guests had gone. The catering staff had packed up. Inside the house, Anaïs slept in her crib, surrounded by family who had insisted on staying to help with the morning-after cleanup.

The vineyard stretched out before us, silver in the moonlight.

"Happy?" Rascon asked, his arm around my shoulders and my head against his chest.

"I didn't know I could be this happy. I didn't know it was possible."

"Get used to it, Mrs. Avila." He pressed a kiss to the top of my head. "This is just the beginning."

I tilted my face up to his, and he kissed me properly. Slow and deep and thorough, the kind of kiss that was a promise and a vow and a commitment all wrapped into one. The kind of kiss that said *forever* without needing words. I'd been wrong when I thought it was the kind that only happened in books and movies. My husband's kiss was all real, and it was all mine.

Keep reading for a sneak peek

at the first book in Heather Slade's

Wicked Winemakers Russian River Valley

First Label series,

Bas' Blend

He let her walk away once.
He won't make that mistake again.
She has three rules for protecting her heart,
and he's already breaking them all.
Together, they're playing with fire,
but neither wants to stop.

BAS

She walked away from me at a wedding, and I haven't stopped thinking about her since. Gemma sees straight through my charm and couldn't care less about my family name—which is exactly why I can't let her go. Hiring her to plan my wine society's events guarantees she'll be close, but she's made the rules crystal clear: professional boundaries only. The problem is, every moment with her makes me want to tear those boundaries down, and I'm terrified that if I push too hard, she'll walk away for good.

GEMMA

I swore off charming, wealthy men after the last one destroyed me. Sebastian Whitmore is everything I promised myself I'd never fall for again—confident, relentless, and far too used to getting what he wants. Working with him is a mistake I made with my eyes wide open, and now I'm spending every day fighting an attraction that threatens to undo three years of carefully rebuilt walls. He makes me want things I'd convinced myself I didn't need anymore, and that terrifies me more than anything.

1

Gemma

I had three rules when it came to working weddings.

Don't get emotionally involved. Don't drink on the job. And never, under any circumstances, let a charming man with a devastating smile convince you that you're any different from any other woman he's met in his lifetime.

Sebastian Whitmore tested all three within five minutes of meeting me.

It was late in the reception—that golden hour when the formal events were finished and guests had loosened their ties and kicked off their heels. The Avila wedding had been beautiful, albeit chaotic. A candle fire, a missing caterer, a flower girl rebellion, and one very determined grandmother, who'd insisted on making a toast despite not being on the schedule. I'd handled all of it with the calm efficiency that had built my reputation.

Now, I stood near the bar, checking items off my list and pretending I didn't notice him approaching.

I'd been aware of Sebastian Whitmore all day. It was hard not to be. He was one of those men who commanded attention without trying—tall, dark-haired, with the kind of easy confidence that came from growing up wealthy and wanted. I'd watched him during dinner, making the rounds and charming every person he spoke to. I'd watched him watching me, too, though I'd pretended not to notice.

Now, he was done watching from a distance.

"You look like you could use this."

I turned to find him holding two glasses of wine, one extended toward me. Up close, he was even more dangerous than I'd anticipated. He had deep brown eyes with laugh lines at the corners, a mouth that tilted up on one side like he was always on the verge of a private joke, and the kind of face that had probably been getting him out of trouble since childhood.

"I don't drink on the job," I said, turning back to my tablet.

"Not even a sip?" He didn't seem deterred. If anything, my dismissal seemed to interest him more. "This is from our reserve collection. Most people would kill for a taste."

"Most people aren't responsible for making sure the sparkler send-off doesn't cause *another* fire."

He laughed—a warm, rich sound that I somehow managed to ignore. Or at least make him think I did.

"Fair enough." He set the rejected glass on the bar and took a sip from his own. "I'm Bas, by the way. Sebastian Whitmore."

"I know who you are."

"Ah." That half smile again. "My reputation precedes me."

"Your name was on the guest list." I finally looked up, letting him see exactly how unimpressed I was. "I make it a point to know who's who."

"And what did your research tell you about me?"

"Research? No. Just awareness." It was a lie. I had looked into the eldest Whitmore when Isabel mentioned they'd been childhood friends. He was the heir to Whitmore Estate, whose father had recently retired. But there was more, which I decided him hearing might take him down a peg. "You date models and actresses, none of whom seem to last more than a few months." I smiled, the polite version I reserved for difficult vendors and handsy groomsmen. "Shall I continue?"

Something shifted in his expression. The easy charm flickered, replaced by something sharper. More real.

"You've done your homework."

"I told you. I make it a point to know who I'm working with." I bit my tongue, wishing I could take my words back the moment I said them—who's who, was what I told him a few seconds ago.

"Is that what we're doing?" He leaned against the bar, close enough that I caught his scent. It was intoxicating. "Working together?"

"The wedding's almost over, Mr. Whitmore. So, no. After tonight, I doubt we'll see each other again."

"Bas," he corrected. "And I wouldn't be so sure about that."

Before I could respond, my headset crackled with a question from the catering manager. I turned away to handle it, and when I glanced over my shoulder, he was gone.

I told myself the twinge of disappointment I felt was just fatigue.

Six weeks later, he walked into my office.

No appointment. No warning. Just Sebastian Whitmore filling my doorway like he owned the place, wearing a jacket that probably cost more than my monthly rent.

"We need to talk," he said.

I set my pen down with deliberate calm. "Most people call ahead."

"I'm not most people."

"No." I leaned back in my chair and studied him. "You're a man who's used to barging into other people's offices, making demands, and leaving after getting what you want. I don't work that way."

"Not the slightest bit interested in why I'm here?"

I was. But I'd never actually tell him that. I folded my arms and looked at my watch. "You have five minutes."

He stepped inside and closed the door behind him. The office suddenly felt smaller, the air thicker. I watched him take in the space—the neat stacks of contracts on my desk, the vision boards covering one wall, the awards displayed on a shelf I'd built myself.

"You're good at what you do," he said.

"I am."

"The Avila wedding was flawless. I've been to a lot of events, Gemma. That one was different. It was personal. Like you actually cared."

"I care about all my events."

"No, you don't." He turned to face me, and the directness in his gaze caught me off guard. "You're professional. Meticulous. But most of the time, you keep your distance. I watched you that night. You were different with Isabel. With the family. Like you'd let them in."

My throat tightened. He wasn't wrong. Isabel and her husband—along with his family—had gotten under my skin in ways I hadn't expected. His mother's warmth. His sister's fierce loyalty. The way they'd absorbed Isabel into their chaos like she'd always belonged there.

It had reminded me of things I'd lost. Things I'd convinced myself I didn't need anymore.

"What do you want, Bas?"

"I want to hire you."

I blinked. "For what?"

"I'm launching something new at Whitmore. A membership program—the 1934 Society. Exclusive events, private tastings, behind-the-scenes access. I need someone to design and execute the signature events." He paused. "I want that someone to be you."

"I'm sure you have a team who can handle all of that."

"I want you."

"Why?"

He took a step closer. Then another. Until he was standing on my side of the desk, close enough that I had to tilt my head back to meet his eyes.

"Because you're the best. Because you don't take shortcuts and you don't settle for mediocre. Because when you commit to something, you give it everything you have." His voice dropped. "And because I haven't been able to stop thinking about you since the night of the wedding, when you walked away from me."

My heart was beating too fast, and I hated the flush I knew was creeping up my neck.

"I don't date clients."

"I'm not asking you to date me. I'm asking you to work with me." That half smile appeared again, but there was an edge to it now. A challenge. "Unless you don't think you can handle it."

"I can handle anything."

"Prove it."

I should have said no. Every instinct I'd honed over the past three years—every lesson I'd learned from the wreckage of my last relationship—screamed at me to refuse. Sebastian Whitmore was exactly the kind of man I'd sworn off. Wealthy. Charming. Used to getting what he wanted. The kind of man who consumed women whole and left nothing behind but ashes.

But there was something in his eyes that gave me pause. Something beneath the confidence and the charm that looked almost vulnerable. Like he was holding his breath, waiting for my answer. Like it actually mattered.

"I'll need creative control," I heard myself say. "No interference, no second-guessing. If I'm doing this, I'm doing it my way."

"Done."

"And clear professional boundaries. Whatever you think is happening here"—I gestured between us—"isn't."

"If you say so."

"I do say so."

He smiled then, a real smile that transformed his face and made something flutter in my chest.

"Then, I guess we have a deal." He extended his hand.

I looked at it. At him. Knowing I was making a mistake but doing it anyway. "Deal."

His palm was warm against mine, his grip firm. He held on a beat longer than necessary, his thumb brushing across my knuckles in a touch so light I almost convinced myself I'd imagined it.

"I'll have my attorney send over a contract," he said. "We can meet at the estate next week to discuss our vision."

"Our?"

"Mine and Isabel's. Well, Kick's too." He released my hand and stepped back, and I could breathe again.

I hated that he'd gotten me to agree without his having to play that particular trump card.

"One more thing." He paused at the door, looking back over his shoulder. "When I said I haven't been able to stop thinking about you since you walked away from me?"

"What about it?"

"You assumed I'm not used to women doing that." His eyes held mine. "I am. In fact, they do it all the time. They're just not the one I want to stay."

He was gone before I could respond.

I sat there, staring at the empty doorway, my hand still tingling where he'd touched it.

I was in trouble.

Deep, dangerous, inevitable trouble.

And the worst part? Some reckless, long-buried part of me couldn't wait to see what happened next.

About the Author

USA Today best-selling author Heather Slade writes shamelessly sexy, edge-of-your seat romantic suspense.

She gave herself the gift of writing a book for her own birthday one year. Sixty-plus books later (and counting), she's having the time of her life.

The women Slade writes are self-confident, strong, with wills of their own, and hearts as big as the Colorado sky. The men are sublimely sexy, seductive alphas who rise to the challenge of capturing the sweet soul of a woman whose heart they'll hold in the palm of their hand forever. Add in a couple of neck-snapping twists and turns, a page-turning mystery, and a swoon-worthy HEA, and you'll be holding one of her books in your hands.

She loves to hear from her readers. You can contact her at heather@heatherslade.com

To keep up with her latest news and releases, please visit her website at www.heatherslade.com to sign up for her newsletter.

MORE FROM AUTHOR HEATHER SLADE

ROMANTIC SUSPENSE

K19 SECURITY
SOLUTIONS
TEAM ONE
Razor's Edge
Gunner's Redemption
Mistletoe's Magic
Mantis' Desire
Dutch's Salvation

K19 SECURITY
SOLUTIONS
TEAM TWO
Striker's Choice
Monk's Fire
Halo's Oath
Tackle's Honor
Onyx's Awakening

K19 SHADOW
OPERATIONS
TEAM ONE
Code Name: Ranger
Code Name: Diesel
Code Name: Wasp
Code Name: Cowboy
Code Name: Mayhem

K19 ALLIED
INTELLIGENCE
TEAM ONE
Code Name: Ares
Code Name: Cayman
Code Name: Poseidon
Code Name: Zeppelin
Code Name: Magnet

K19 ALLIED
INTELLIGENCE
TEAM TWO
Code Name: Puck
*Code Name:
Michelangelo*
Code Name: Typhon
Code Name: Hornet
Code Name: Reaper

K19 GENESIS
CONSORTIUM
TEAM ONE
Blackjack's Ascent
Dagger's Shield
Sundance's Trail
Nomad's Compass
Preacher's Decree

K19 SENTINEL
CYBER
TEAM ONE
Code Name: Admiral
Code Name: Dante
Code Name: Grit
Code Name: Tank
Code Name: Atticus

K19 SENTINEL
CYBER
TEAM TWO
Code Name: Kodiak
Code Name: Paragon
Code Name: Vex
Code Name: Shredder
Code Name: Jagger

PROTECTORS
UNDERCOVER
TEAM ONE
Undercover Agent
Undercover Emissary
Undercover Savior
Undercover Infidel
Undercover Shadow

ROYAL AGENTS
OF MI6
Make Me Shiver
Drive Me Wilder
Feel My Pinch
Chase My Shadow
Find My Angel

THE INVINCIBLES
TEAM ONE
Code Name: Deck
Code Name: Edge
Code Name: Grinder
Code Name: Rile
Code Name: Smoke

THE INVINCIBLES
TEAM TWO
Code Name: Buck
Code Name: Irish
Code Name: Saint
Code Name: Hammer
Code Name: Rip

THE
UNSTOPPABLES
TEAM ONE
Code Name: Fury
Code Name: Merried

MORE FROM AUTHOR HEATHER SLADE

WINE COUNTRY ROMANCE

BUTLER RANCH
Kade's Worth
Brodie's Promise
Maddox's Truce
Naughton's Secret
Mercer's Vow
Kade's Return
Butler Ranch Christmas

**WICKED WINEMAKERS
CENTRAL COAST
FIRST LABEL**
Brix's Bid
Ridge's Release
Press' Passion
Zin's Sins
Tryst's Temptation

**WICKED WINEMAKERS
CENTRAL COAST
SECOND LABEL**
Beau's Beloved
Cru's Crush
Bit's Bliss
Snapper's Seduction
Kick's Kiss

**WICKED WINEMAKERS
RUSSIAN RIVER VALLEY
FIRST LABEL**
Bas' Blend
Hux's Harvest
Wolf's Want
Oak's Vintage
Cooper's Claim

COWBOY ROMANCE

**COWBOYS OF
CRESTED BUTTE**
A Cowboy Falls
A Cowboy's Dance
A Cowboy's Kiss
A Cowboy Stays
A Cowboy Wins

ROARING FORK RANCH
Roaring Fork Wrangler
Roaring Fork Roughstock
Roaring Fork Rockstar
Roaring Fork Rooker
Roaring Fork Bridger

SANGRE VISTA RANCH
Thorn's Stand
Stetson's Storm
Maverick's Reckoning
Cinch's Wager
Flints Chance